A DANCE WITH THE DEVIL

FINDING NEVERLAND

Printed in the United States of America: First Printing, 2022
ISBN 978-1-7351315-5-9 (paperback)

Published by Night Muse Press
Cover Art by Maria Spada Design
Edited by The Word Faery
Proofread by Fantasy Proofs
Illustrated by Nathan Hansen Illustration
Formatted by R. L. Davennor

NIGHT MUSE PRESS
EST. 2020

Acknowledgements

To Jena – duh.
To Elora, whose encouragement was as
valuable as your help with Spanish.
To Lisette, who believed in my ability
to make flesh-eating sirens sexy.
To the lovely ladies of Midwinter Magic
who helped bring this story to life.
To my readers, who all but demanded
more Cedric in their lives.
And to my pirate king and queen,
who saved me yet again. I will never
tire of writing your story.

Also by R. L. Davennor:

The Curses of Never Series:

A Land of Never After

A Sea of Eternal Woe – Coming Summer 2022

Others:

Dragon Lake: A Swan Lake Retelling

Lyres, Legends, and Lullabies: An Annotated Score Collection

To the Crow. One day, very soon, you'll find your wings.

Content Warning:

This novella contains graphic depictions of violence, language, explicit sexual content, spicy, often stabby banter, and is intended for a mature adult audience.

Here there be pirates, and they speak and act accordingly.

One girl is more use than twenty boys.
    - J. M. Barrie, *Peter Pan*

I. THE ESCAPE

I'd fucked up. Severely.

    I knew it each time a rat skittered across my feet, felt it each time an icy drop of liquid struck my forehead. I swore my captors had positioned me here on purpose, where the ceiling leaked a constant stream of water. At least . . . I hoped it was water.

Gritting my teeth and swallowing the string of obscenities I wanted badly to utter, I tested the manacles that kept me fastened to the stone wall. The unforgiving iron bit into my sensitive flesh, holding firm as ever. I ignored the sting. Compared to the rot constantly eating away at my innards—my curse—it was nothing, and for once, I was grateful for the dull pain. It gave me something to focus on other than my racing thoughts. If I were an intelligent man, I'd be fixated on saving my own skin, or at the very least, fighting off the curse that would kill me if I wasn't careful, but I'd proven time and time again that I wasn't. I wouldn't be here if I was, literally rotting away in this lonely cell while Scarlett endured far worse at the hands of Admiral Diego Ruiz.

Scarlett. A lump formed in my throat, one I couldn't swallow, as her terrified gaze flashed across my mind. That look she'd given me before being dragged away was one that would haunt me for the rest of my days, however numbered they may have been. How had it come to this? Only two nights ago, we'd been huddled in my quarters, our bodies pressed so close together it had been impossible to imagine anyone ever tearing us apart.

Then he arrived—the Devil himself.

Unrestrained rage clouded my thoughts, and red streaked across my vision. I wasn't scared of Ruiz's theatrical nickname. What I wouldn't give to rip that bastard limb from limb, slice his cock off before shoving it raw and bloody down—

"Shame. I heard it's quite big."

I sucked in a breath but needn't have bothered; the voice was all too familiar. "*Elvira?*"

"Feliz Navidad, hermano."

"It's not Navidad yet," I snapped back, still unsure as to where the voice was coming from.

"Soon enough." A blade glittered in the darkness, quickly followed by my sister's smirking face. I almost shuddered; how long had she been lurking in the shadows, letting me sit in my own piss? "You know, as entertaining as they are, you really should be more careful about your vengeful mutterings. What if a real guard had overheard you?" Elvira stood dressed in one of their uniforms—well, half-dressed. It had either been sloppily donned, or she'd gotten here by seducing everyone she passed. I'd normally be willing to bet the latter, but even in the dimly lit cell, I could tell she was covered in enough blood to shock anyone but a fellow pirate.

I raised an eyebrow. "You're one to talk. Seems as though you had your own fun."

Elvira snorted. "I don't need to be cursed to enjoy slitting throats. Especially Navy ones—they're always so pretty. Practically begging for it." Whipping out a set of keys, she began fiddling with the lock to my cell; the medallion shard draped around her neck bounced as she worked. "Don't worry. I saved a few for you."

I shot her a glare. My curse was certainly a problem, but it remained the least of my worries. "You took your damn time, and we can't afford it. Scarlett is still—"

"Scarlett? Look at yourself. Have they even fed you, Ced?"

They hadn't, and the rot was ravaging me at a much faster rate than normal as a result, but I couldn't tell Elvira that. "Yes."

"That's a lie. You always get that crease in your forehead when you tell one."

"I'm *fine.*"

"I'll be the judge of that." A click, and my cell door swung open. Elvira knelt by my side, wrinkling her nose disapprovingly. "You

3

smell like shit."

"You smell like death," I snapped but silenced abruptly when my sister's hand wormed its way beneath what little fabric remained of my shirt. Her palm was icy against my fever-hot chest, but more than that, it fueled my discomfort. Only Scarlett ever touched me skin to skin, and for good reason; it was how the curse spread. "What are you doing?"

Elvira ignored me, quickly moving farther down my body until she reached my pockets. Finding nothing, she shot me a fierce glare. "Do not tell me you were wearing Lucas's shard."

Gods, the damn shard. Each of my siblings possessed a piece of the same medallion, and so long as they wore it, they were shielded from the effects of our father's curse. I swallowed. "I—"

"Don't tell me that you *lost* it."

"All right—I didn't lose it. Ruiz *took* it before they put me in here."

Elvira cursed in Spanish, all but spitting in my face. "He's got a shard?"

"He's got Scarlett!" I leaned forward as much as I was able, given that I remained fastened to the wall, only barely managing not to shout. "I don't give a fuck about that damn trinket until we have her back." Having already been infected, it offered me no protection.

Barely contained rage saturated Elvira's whisper. "That 'damn trinket' cost us three years of our lives. Men died—our *brother* died—for us to secure it." She yanked on the cord around her neck, holding up her own medallion shard for me to see. A serpent stared back, fangs bared and body coiled to strike. "And you didn't take it off before the *Spanish Navy* raided our ship?"

"No—because I was too busy wondering where the three of you had fucked off to!" Unable to hold back my fury, I yanked on my manacles, reopening wounds I barely felt at the moment. "I woke up to chaos, the crew was in hysterics, and all of you were gone." I didn't have to specify; Elvira would know I meant her, Scarlett, and my quartermaster, Adrian. "Nowhere to be found. Next thing I know, Ruiz had boarded us, Scarlett is a captive, and the two of you had abandoned ship like cowards. They even knew not to touch my skin, treated me like a leper. They knew all about the curse, so unless they're fucking psychic, someone told them everything." I met her harrowed gaze. "Are you ready to explain *that* to me?"

Silence.

"Let me know when you are. Until then, fuck off about the damn shard."

Elvira reached up to unlock my manacles. While she searched for the right key, she released a breath against my forehead. "If it weren't for us cowards, you'd have met the noose by now."

I ignored that. "Where's Adrian?"

"Waiting with horses outside. I only had to kill a dozen or so guards to reach you. You know, for as badly as the Devil wanted you prisoner, I really expected more of a challenge in breaking you out."

So had I, to be honest, and wasn't certain what to make of such an easy success. Elvira may have been as deadly as a viper, but even she could be bested if enough competent men were standing guard. Either we'd been wildly underestimated, which was just plain insulting, or we were playing right into Ruiz's hands. Both scenarios boiled my blood, and I couldn't stifle the animalistic snarl that sounded from my lips. I couldn't wait until I heard that whoreson *scream*—

"You can craft your revenge later." For the second time, Elvira's voice tore me from my murderous thoughts as my manacles clicked open. *Or did I speak aloud again?* "We have to move."

"Right." Rubbing my aching wrists, I nodded before staggering to my feet. Pushing through the dizziness that rushed to my forehead, I closely followed my sister's lead. Once free of the grimy cell, she passed me an unsheathed dagger without looking back or stopping. I hesitated, but of course, Elvira anticipated my reaction.

"Fuck's sake, Ced," she hissed. "A gun would be far too noisy. Knives are the only option."

Stifling a curse of my own, I took the weapon, already loathing the way the pommel felt in my hands. It wasn't that I didn't know how to wield a blade—far from it—I'd simply had one turned against me too many times. Bullets were cleaner and more efficient in most cases. Unfortunately, this wasn't one of them.

"Go for the throat, sever the vocal cords. We don't want them screaming."

Elvira didn't wait for me to reply before setting off again. She had an uncanny knack for slithering through darkness; they didn't call her the Serpent for nothing. I found it difficult to match her stealth but did my best as we rounded corner after corner, tearing down the longer halls at a reckless sprint if we could see that they were already clear. More than once, I nearly tripped over the bodies marking our way, and each time, Elvira's arm shot out to steady me.

She halted after the third, brows knotting in concern. "Are you sure you're—"

"Fine," I lied. "Keep moving." I didn't know what I was, but *fine* certainly wasn't the right answer; beyond obvious dehydration and a curse eating me alive, I hadn't slept since the last night I'd spent with Scarlett. I'd woken just after midnight to cannon fire, to see Admiral Ruiz's ship much too close to our own. There'd been no plausible route of escape, and the battle had ended before it even began. *The Jolly Serpent* was captured, and my surviving men were rounded up like cattle, chained up like dogs—all except Elvira and Adrian: cowards or saviors, I still hadn't decided.

And all except for Scarlett, whose chains weren't literal.

This time, I swallowed the rage I'd summoned. *You'll get her back*, I assured myself. *She's alive. He wanted her alive.* The knowledge filled me with a conflicting mixture of comfort and fury, but mostly the former when I pictured Scarlett putting to good use everything I'd taught her. If there was anything I *did* know for certain, it was that she wouldn't go down without a fight.

Neither would my men, I hoped, but what had become of them? "The others," I murmured. Now wasn't the time to hold a conversation, but I needed to know. "Where have they imprisoned the others?" It wasn't here, and that much had been clear during my initial capture. They'd separated me from the rest, I'd originally assumed so they could kill me without witnesses who might inform Scarlett of my fate.

Elvira didn't answer, and given the slight tilt of her head, she'd heard me.

"Our *crew*, Elvira. Three dozen good men and boys. I know they tossed me in here alone, but surely they're all—"

"There," came Elvira's sigh of relief, completely disregarding my question. Ahead, filtering through a narrow crevice, were flickers of dim light. "Adrian should be—"

Movement caught the corner of my eye, but my lips barely moved fast enough. "*Duck!*"

She did just in time, though because of my warning or her reflexes, I couldn't be certain. Elvira's assailant swore before recovering from his miss, setting his sights on me instead. He held a knife. *Fuck.*

"Going somewhere, Teach?" the guard growled, his heavy Spanish accent making my skin crawl. He nursed a bloodied shoulder and a bad limp, but impressively, raised his blade. "I'd reconsider. Heard Ruiz and his bride already fucking like dogs."

I stilled. Fist clenching around my own dagger, I became unable to picture anything but what the guard had described. "She wouldn't go anywhere near him." Not willingly, anyway.

"Are you sure about that?" The guard stalked closer, releasing a low chuckle. "We expected you to be stupid, but not this stupid."

"He touches her, *he's* as good as dead." I shouldn't have been playing that game, but it was too late to pretend I didn't care. "Scarlett is cursed just like me. The slightest brush of skin to skin and you catch it."

"Cedric," Elvira warned. She remained at a distance but eyed both of us warily. "End this."

"We know. We know everything." Ignoring her, the guard continued his advance; a few more steps and he'd force my back to the prison wall. Like the men who had attacked our ship, he was dressed neck to toe in clothing thick enough to ensure my touch wouldn't endanger him. "About the curse, the shards, your fear of knives, all of it. Wouldn't you like to know how?"

My skin prickled uncomfortably. This man may have been succeeding in getting a rise out of me, but beyond that, he had a point. How *did* Ruiz's men know exactly how to sneak up on us, all about the curse Scarlett and I shared, and how it worked? How had a battle which should have lasted hours been over before it even began?

What was Elvira not telling me?

"Look at you." He was in my face now, so close I could smell the stench on his breath. Raising the knife to my throat, he laughed again when I inhaled sharply. "A cowardly, sniveling cr—"

His insult became lost in a gurgle of blood. Slumping, he soon collapsed, and only then did I see another blade protruding from the back of his neck.

"Puto cabrón," Elvira spat as she yanked it out.

I raised an eyebrow. "Was that for me or him?"

"You." She narrowed her gaze. "He should have been *your* kill. Gods know you need one."

The twinge in my gut was the ever-present reminder that I did. Spilling blood was the only way to satisfy the curse, and doing so would both temporarily heal me and slow my rot for a time. But without fail, it always crept back . . . and I swore it was accelerating as fast as it seemed to be spreading. I feigned nonchalance. "I'll find another."

"You'd better." Without sparing me a glance, Elvira nodded toward the exit. "Keep moving."

Normally, I'd have obeyed, especially at a time like this, but the air had chilled around us—literally *and* figuratively. Elvira had gone stiff, and it had nothing to do with the corpse lying between us. I decided to meet her head-on. "There's something you're not telling me. What's—"

"Later." She still wouldn't look at me. "Trust me, Cedric . . . now's not the time."

She was probably right, but that didn't quell the rage kindling within me, and neither did her use of my full name. Elvira only called me Cedric when she was serious, and she was never serious. "Does this have anything to do with—"

"I said *later*."

Not wanting to be detained any further, I followed, this time paying much closer attention to our surroundings. We weren't stopped again, and it wasn't long before cool air wafted from the haphazard crevice that was our destination. I may have sighed in relief had a disturbing realization not struck me. "It's night?"

Elvira nodded, extending a hand to me for balance as I navigated my way through the opening apparently carved with nothing but hammers and pickaxes; the evidence lay all around us. "Five days until Navidad."

Shit. I hadn't spent one night captive, but two. It explained the delay in my rescue, given the hole they'd had to carve, and no wonder I was so damned hungry and exhausted.

"The Crow emerges! Underground never was any place to keep a bird."

I turned toward the familiar voice. Too exhausted to protest being called by my shitty nickname, I nodded a stiff greeting toward the other half of Elvira's cowardice. "That dip in the sea didn't give your old bones frostbite?"

Adrian laughed off my attempt at a jab. "Gonna take more than that to kill the likes o' me. But what 'bout you—are ya hurt? Did they take the flog to ya?" Before I could protest, my quartermaster yanked at my shirt, evidently to check for fresh wounds.

"Careful," I hissed, not wanting to accidentally touch him. I pulled my shirt from his grasp and backed away, trying and failing to hide my still-bleeding wrists. "No. I'm fine."

"And I'd still be in there flaying those men alive if they'd harmed him," Elvira added. "He'll need a kill, though. Had an opportunity a while back but missed it."

I shot her a glare. "I didn't miss it, you just got impatient."

"No. Demasiado lento."

"English," I snapped. I knew some Spanish thanks to Scarlett, but that was exactly the problem—the language reminded me of her. And until she was back in my arms, I didn't want to think about the ones currently holding her prisoner.

Adrian cleared his throat. "You two finished? We've places ta—"

"We're very much not." I stood my ground, determined to

uncover whatever my sister was hiding. Perhaps the third inquiry would be the charm. "*Now* will you tell me where they are?"

She snapped her mouth shut, rendered speechless for once. It only enraged me further.

"What's the fucking problem?" I all but bellowed. "Where is *The Jolly Serpent*? Where are my men?" I took a step forward, but Adrian stepped into my path.

"*Hush*. Do ya want the Devil himself to hear ya?"

"I'd welcome the literal devil if he gave me answers," I snarled, resisting the urge to push Adrian aside only because of my curse. "I'll not give the men even further reason to distrust me as captain. For fuck's sake, where *are* they?" Beyond that, rescuing them was the right thing to do, but I didn't say that part aloud. They already thought me far too soft—present company included.

Elvira shook her head, hissing through her teeth. "Ced, you don't—"

"They're dead," Adrian said bluntly. "Hanged."

Even the wind quieted down, mirroring the shock that rippled through me. "What?" I glanced between my sister and quartermaster, but neither offered a response to my disbelief. Men had died in the brief struggle with the Admiral, I knew, and it wasn't as though Ruiz had any reason to keep them prisoner for long—but to slaughter an entire crew in a single day? There'd been boys among them, for Adais's sake. Weight settled atop my already constricted chest, but I forced the words from my throat. "All of them?"

Elvira shook her head. She opened her mouth, attempting to form words, but nothing ever came out.

"Cedric." Adrian alone seemed capable of coherent speech. "The rest were sold into slavery and loaded onto cargo ships last night. They'll be halfway 'cross the Caribbean by now, likely headed to British colonies on the mainland."

Halfway . . . across the Caribbean? As slaves?

Gods *fucking* damn it.

We were miles from the sea, but it was as though a wave had washed over me, only it didn't engulf me with water; it engulfed me with rage. Scarlett, my freedom, and my ship evidently hadn't been enough. The Devil had also taken it upon himself to steal the lives of my men. My crew.

My life.

I hadn't realized I'd gone to punch the prison wall until Elvira stopped my blow in its tracks. With a knowing look, she lowered my arm, speaking for my ears alone. "A broken hand isn't going to help you rescue Scarlett."

"You suddenly give a shit about her?" I snapped before I could help myself.

Elvira narrowed her gaze. "I care about *you* and know you won't rest until she's safe. Besides," she added, fingers grazing my chest right where the rot was at its worst; I was too exhausted to push her away. "If we're going to break your curse, we need that shard."

"Ya lost the shard?" Adrian butted in, jaw parted in disbelief. "That wasn't part o' the—"

"We need to get moving," Elvira cut in, gesturing toward the horses tethered a few yards away. There were only two, but that was probably for the best; I wasn't certain I'd be able to hold myself upright in a saddle at the present moment. "There's a tavern not far."

"Won't they be looking for us?" I pointed out. The prison's alarm bells hadn't sounded—Elvira must have taken care of the guards manning those, too—but it wouldn't be long before someone discovered what had happened here. And once word reached Ruiz, it would be a manhunt. "Wouldn't it be safer to travel a bit out of the way?"

"Are you in any condition to?"

My face reddened. "No, but—"

"We'll make do, and I've already paid the barkeep to keep his mouth shut. I know it's been a while since you've needed to hide your face, Cedric, but slip back into the habit quickly."

Adrian tossed me a hooded cloak rather roughly. After donning it, I settled atop the horse behind Elvira, wrapping an arm around her waist as loosely as possible. It didn't keep her from chuckling.

"Don't get too comfortable, hermano."

I rolled my eyes. "Wouldn't dream of it."

Elvira kept her promise, and we didn't ride for long. The streets were quiet and still with no guards in sight as we put up the horses in the tavern's stable; they'd probably already been sent to clean up our mess at the prison. The thought may have made me smile had I not still been consumed with worry for Scarlett. I had little doubt she was with Ruiz right now. I'd seen the way he looked at her, heard what he'd said to her the moment he was certain I was within earshot.

"*Te echado de menos, mi desposada.*"

14

My Spanish wasn't as good as Elvira's, but I knew what Ruiz had called Scarlett: *my bride*. Her engagement to the Admiral was the life she'd fled prior to ending up aboard my ship, and the ghost she'd been running from ever since. Ruiz had been tracking us for months, determined to rescue Scarlett from the pirates that had allegedly kidnapped her, as well as see me hanged for corrupting his precious noblewoman.

I gritted my teeth. It was true that one of us would hang, but not that it would be me. And Scarlett was no noblewoman, whether Ruiz wanted to believe it or not. She'd been raised in the brothels of Spain by her courtesan mother prior to the woman's death, and only then had Scarlett's English father—the late Lieutenant Robert Maynard—stepped in as her caretaker, shipping her across the Atlantic to the Caribbean colonies to better keep an eye on her. Scarlett never quite took to her new life of corsets and embroidery, but it wasn't until her engagement that she finally ran away from that life . . . of her own free will, I might add. I may have been many things, but a kidnapper wasn't one of them.

I remained lost in thought as we entered the tavern at the back. After bypassing the busy bar and the hordes of Navidad decorations scattered about, we headed straight for the room Adrian had secured for us. The hall wasn't deserted, but we dodged everyone easily enough—until we didn't. Elvira halted so suddenly I nearly slammed into her stiff back; before I could protest, a stranger beat me to it.

"Going somewhere, cariño?"

It was my turn to tense as the man blocking our way reached

behind my sister's ear, twirling a strand of her golden hair between his fingers. Adrian stood behind him, watching us warily, and with a jolt, I realized why. The stranger was dressed in a guard's uniform, wearing Ruiz's colors. My heart dropped to my knees as the guard prodded again.

"I haven't seen you around here before. Are you new?"

He must have thought Elvira was a prostitute, and I could hardly blame him. She had shed her stolen uniform prior to us departing the prison, and the little she still had on didn't exactly leave much to the imagination. Her tattered skirt sported a long slit, exposing her legs, and her top didn't cover much more than her breasts. I bit my lip to keep from swearing, gaze flickering to Adrian for guidance.

Elvira fired something back in Spanish, saving us both from coming up with a response. I seized the opportunity to yank my hood down even farther. *Please let us pass,* please *let us pass*—

The guard's gaze flickered to Adrian and me before fixating back on Elvira. "¿Vas a venir a mi cama cuando termines con esos perdedores?" he asked.

"Por supuesto." Elvira flashed him a coy smile. Gods, was it over? I'd know what they were saying if I were paying better attention, but Spanish evaded me when stressed.

Apparently, it wasn't. "¿Puedo probar?"

"Sírvete."

Adrian came to my rescue just as the guard smothered my poor sister, sloppily kissing her in a way that made me want to vomit. Those noises . . . Was he *actually* sucking on her face?

I grimaced and shook off Adrian's gloved grip, speaking only once we were farther down the hall and out of earshot. "Is she all right? Do we need to—"

"Ya really need to work on yer Spanish, especially here," Adrian snapped. "Elvira's fine—playing into his little fantasy. No idea why, but it's not as if she can't take care of herself. Now, get yer ass inside before someone sees yer scars."

I didn't need to be told twice. While Adrian waited by the door for Elvira to catch up, I wasted no time stripping free of both that awful cloak and my ruined shirt, breathing a sigh of relief as cool air caressed my aching skin. There rested a bucket of clean water in the corner, and I used it to sponge off. I'd finished tending my wounded wrists and moved to my rotting abdomen just as Elvira ducked inside, grinning from ear to ear.

I gagged upon recalling that awful kiss. "How can you be smiling after that?"

"Because I just solved all our problems."

"All of them?" Adrian crossed his arms. "That's a tall order."

"What can I say? I'm efficient *and* thorough." Elvira raised her chin, still looking smug.

I narrowed my gaze. She hadn't been gone long, but with my sister, anything was possible. "Sex never solves anything, especially sex involving you."

Elvira's lips parted; now, she did look offended. "I don't need to resort to sex to get a man's clothes off." Whipping out a bundle from behind her back, she tossed it in my direction. The clothes tumbled just short of me, landing in a crumpled heap on the floor. The guard's uniform.

I gaped. "What did you—"

"He thinks I'm fucking you two and wants next in line. I told him to be ready and waiting—so he stripped. Eagerly, I might add."

Adrian doubled over laughing, but I gritted my teeth. I'd just escaped one prison and had no plans to land myself in another. "You think this is funny? We're supposed to be lying low, not robbing Ruiz's men."

"It's not robbing. It's borrowing—you can give it back once you're done." Elvira shot me a glare. "But if you'd like to get into El Diablo's mansion the hard way, I'll just be taking it back—"

"Wait—no." My exhausted mind worked to piece together what she'd implied. "These are for me?"

"To pose as a guard, Ced, yes. Are you certain they didn't drop you on your head before they strung you up?"

Before I could snap a retort, Adrian beat me to it. "And that unfortunate lad won't talk, because he won't want to admit to gettin' seduced by a tavern wench." He nodded approvingly. "I'm impressed, Elvira."

"Don't thank me yet," she warned. "Ced's scars stand out too much. He'll need one hell of a convincing disguise if he wants any chance of getting anywhere near Scarlett, and honestly, I don't know if that uniform will be enough. He's likely to need something for his face."

"Are ya certain?" Adrian questioned. "I've seen the mansion

guards' armor—they're covered head to toe, I'm assuming to prevent themselves from being cursed—"

Scarlett.

They kept talking, but I wasn't listening. A single truth consumed my thoughts: one way or another, this nightmare would be over soon.

"Mi amor," I whispered, clutching the still-warm uniform like it was a lifeline pulling me to shore. "I'm *coming.*"

II. THE PLOT

"Fuck, this itches."

"And you think mine doesn't?" I shot Elvira a glare through the slit in my guard's helmet, but she wasn't looking at me. She continued rifling through the endless layers of her handmaid's petticoat, seemingly searching for the source of her discomfort. It had been damn near ten minutes since we'd passed ourselves off as a shift change and boarded the carriage taking us to the Devil's seaside mansion, and in all that time, she didn't appear to have even reached her legs. I rolled my eyes. "The only way you'll feel better is when you take it off—"

"I'd *love* to."

"—and it's going to be a long day," I finished flatly. "So will you quit squirming and at least try to sit like a lady? You'll incriminate us before we've even gotten inside."

"The day I 'sit like a lady' is the day hell freezes over."

She had a point, so I shut up for the time being; just as well, for my mind needed steeling. Adrian wasn't here to talk sense into me— he'd stayed behind to listen to the whispers back at the tavern and to intervene in case anything went wrong—and even the ever-present pain from my curse wasn't enough of a distraction on its own. There was part of me that wanted nothing more than to hack and slice my way to Scarlett, felling as many bodies as was necessary to reach her. Each kill would not only fuel me and appease my curse, but each of Ruiz's men I slaughtered would be payback for the lives he'd stolen from me . . . part of it, anyway. As far as I was concerned, no amount of bloodshed would ever replace the loss burning a hole in my chest.

And as much as I was loath to admit it, it wouldn't save Scarlett. It might even get her killed. Ruiz may know this game as well as I did, but even he had limits—push them, and I could lose everything. I wasn't here to even come close. The plan was straightforward. Get in, get Scarlett, and get out. Get in, get Scarlett, and get—

"You're forgetting Lucas's shard. We most certainly cannot leave without it."

I glanced up to see Elvira glaring from her seat opposite me. My cheeks burned; she must think me mad. *Gods, you really must stop muttering your thoughts aloud.* "Yes, yes—the shard, too. I may have simplified the process, but yes, that's more or less how I imagined it would go."

"Do you really think it's going to be that easy? That we'll be able to just waltz in and snatch what we came here for?"

"There will be guards, I'm sure, but we'll make quick work of them." I narrowed my gaze. We'd been in far worse messes before; how was this any different?

Elvira shook her head and groaned. "You imagined wrong, brother. Love may be clouding *your* judgement, but there's no way that's true for Ruiz. Look around."

Without shifting too much, I followed her gaze outside the carriage window.

My heart sank to my knees, for the grounds were absolutely crawling with guards. Like ants, at least a dozen scurried to and fro across the perfectly manicured lawn, while more guarded every visible entrance. Judging from the eye rolls and scowls, this wasn't their normal routine, and there was only one perceived threat to have appeared within the last twenty-four hours—*me*. Apprehension turned to anger, and I barely suppressed a growl. The back half of the mansion overlooked the sea, so the grounds were our only hope; if this was what we had to work with, how on earth were we going to make it to Scarlett?

"It would appear as though El Diablo heard of my escape."

"You think?" Elvira hissed. She yanked the curtain closed before all but throwing herself back into her seat. "We'll need to be careful and on our guard, no matter how 'easy' Ruiz makes this. We don't so much as breathe until we have Scarlett and the shard *and* we're far from this place. We don't get cocky, and we don't act reckless."

Easy for her to say. Elvira was as vengeful as I was, but like a real-life serpent, she was the type to wait in the shadows for the perfect moment before she struck. As the Crow, I held grudges and tended to charge into things without thinking, but that's exactly what had gotten us into this mess. Much as I was loath to admit it, my sister was right. Nothing could be done without thinking it through first.

"How reckless would it be to kill?" I asked, lowering my voice as our carriage approached the inner gates. "At least one. Otherwise, I might fall to pieces." It was an exaggeration, but only just. I hadn't appeased my curse in nearly a week, and there was no concealing the smell of the rot now. Hopefully, anyone who got too close would simply assume I was badly in need of a wash, but the additional attention it would attract wasn't going to aid our mission.

Elvira's expression softened, but only for a moment. "Make it quick. And remember—it'll have to look like an accident, or it's us who are as good as dead. Nothing bloody, and no spectacle."

"That's no fun."

"Ced—"

"Kidding," I lied. "You're right. It's not worth the risk."

She didn't seem as though she believed me, but nodded nonetheless. We rode in silence after that. I inhaled deeply, reminding myself of a single truth: I needed to rein in my rage; now wasn't the time to let it consume me. There was no choice but to be patient.

But the moment it proved necessary, the moment I smelled a rat, there were no limits to what I would do to ensure Scarlett's rescue.

Failure wasn't even an option; the only acceptable outcomes were victory or death, and not just my own. I'd bring this entire fucking mansion down with me.

It would be a true shame if it came to that. Even I couldn't deny that the property was breathtaking and a perfect fit for a Navy Admiral. The mansion hugged a cliffside, with its rear overlooking a sizable beach. Even I could find no fault with the unobstructed view of the open sea. I gazed in its direction, listening hard for the comforting ebb and flow of the tide . . . but picked up something else entirely.

A melody, faint but clear, rose and fell on the breeze. It was subtle as a whisper yet piercing as a scream, and only got more intense the longer I entertained it. I inhaled sharply; I'd heard that song before.

"Elvira," I hissed, kicking her shins.

She cursed. "What?"

"Do you hear that?"

"Nothing other than you being a fool."

"Listen *carefully*." It was there, unmistakable now. Surely, she couldn't miss it. "Siren song."

"I don't hear anything, Ced." Elvira narrowed her gaze, more concerned than annoyed at my insistence. "Especially not sirens. They don't come this close to shore—you know that."

If there was anything this life had taught me, it was that nothing ever went as I expected. Still, it wasn't as if I could do much about the sirens now, even if they *were* there—the moment Elvira had denounced it, the song had died away.

"Sorry," I muttered, shifting away from the window. "Must be hearing things." But despite my best efforts to silence it, the song continued in my head right up until we arrived.

"Ready?" Elvira asked.

"As I'll ever be."

She stood just before the horses stopped, shoving her way from the narrow space before the carriage doors had been opened for us. "Shift change," she announced brusquely, not even sparing the women who had come to greet us a second glance. "We'll just be—"

"Hold on." The older of the two women held out her hand, blocking Elvira's path. I couldn't see my sister's expression through the narrow opening in my helmet, but I didn't miss her hands clench at her sides. "You must be new—I don't recall a face half as pretty as yours. Tell me, lass, how is it you know where you're going?"

I clenched my jaw; I'd warned Elvira that her usual air of confidence wouldn't be enough, not when the mansion staff had no doubt been told to keep an eye out for us. I hadn't wanted to speak so soon but saw no alternative. Stepping in front of her, I cleared my throat. "She's with me. I'm to show her to her assignment."

The handmaids turned to me, and the older one raised a brow. "And why would you do that? The guards' barracks are that way."

Shit. "I—"

"You're right, Señora, I am new. This is my brother, Julián," Elvira answered before I could, smiling widely. "He's worked here for a few weeks and offered to show me around on my first day. Isn't he kind?"

The handmaids nodded, but their gazes remained narrowed.

"Kind, indeed."

"And late. Disculpe, por favor." Snatching Elvira's hand, I pushed my way past the women and into the mansion's lower level, shuddering slightly as cooler air wormed its way between the gaps in my armor. Voices called after us for a brief span of time, but thankfully, we weren't pursued.

Elvira sighed, remaining close as she spoke in a breathy whisper. "That was close."

"Too close," I hissed. "We need to be a lot smarter if we're going to—"

"¡Buenos días!"

I nearly leaped from my skin at the unfamiliar voice, but Elvira wasn't fazed. After returning the greeting, she took over leading the way into a brightly lit room. Dozens of handmaids and their things lay scattered about; most were in various stages of dress, either preparing for or returning from a shift. Thankful for the helmet concealing my reddening cheeks, I did my best not to stare at anything in particular as the person who'd greeted us addressed Elvira, disregarding my presence completely. Unlike the older handmaid we'd encountered at the doors, this one didn't question her new-ness.

"You're just in time to leave with the group. While she's being presented to the guests, Lady Maynard has tasked us with decorating the grand hall for Nochebuena. They've gathered in the halls, so we will need to use the eastern staircase—"

My blood turned to ice at the mention of Scarlett. "Lady Maynard?" I echoed, very much butting into the conversation.

"She's giving . . . orders?"

The handmaid furrowed her brow. "Of course—why would she not?"

I didn't have a coherent answer, given that I could hardly breathe.

"I don't recall requesting additional security." Suspicion clouded the woman's face, and I felt her eyes attempting to pierce my armor. "Where did you come from?"

Elvira tensed beside me and maybe even said something, but I wasn't listening. I wasn't *thinking*. Before I knew it, I'd turned toward the nearest staircase, ignoring the claims that it was blocked before ascending the steps two at a time. I didn't know where I was going, didn't possess a single lead, but I didn't care; I had two things to find. The first was Scarlett, and the second was whatever the fuck was going on, because something wasn't adding up. She was a prisoner. A captive.

But prisoners didn't give orders.

Gods, what is happening? My mind spun, dizzying as it struggled to piece together all I knew. Elvira and Adrian hadn't acted right since the night of my capture, nor had they *during* the capture—running from a fight, especially a fight with the Navy, simply wasn't like them. My sister wouldn't leave my side without damn good reason, and she also wasn't one to evade my questions. Now this? Something was going on, and I was hellbent on discovering exactly what, even if it killed me.

The higher I ascended, the more clamor permeated my chaotic thoughts, and by the time I'd reached the main floor, voices had drowned out my mind completely. I stilled at the sheer mass of people before me, dumbfounded as I took in the crowd. It wasn't even midday, yet bodies were so tightly packed together that those insistent on moving were having difficulty navigating a clear path, because of both the Navidad decorations shoved into every available corner and the people. The vast majority were men dressed in Navy uniforms, though a few well-groomed women stood at what I assumed were their partners' sides. Judging by the excited chatter and frequent glances toward a grand set of doors draped in colored garlands, they seemed to be waiting for something. It didn't take long to find out what.

Almost instantaneously, the massive doors swung open, the murmurs turned to applause. I couldn't tell who'd emerged at first glance, not over the commotion, but as the horde parted to allow them through, I heard a laugh that may as well have been a knife straight through my heart.

Scarlett.

There she stood, smiling bright with her head held high and looking nothing like a prisoner. Rather, she resembled royalty, especially given how she so effortlessly commanded the attention of everyone she passed. Her hair had been braided and her ragged clothes traded for a magnificent emerald gown. That fire in her eyes I loved so much burned brighter than I'd ever seen it, and at her side, seemingly fueling it, stood El Diablo himself. They may not have worn crowns, but that hardly mattered.

They were the king and queen of my own personal hell.

Had I not been gripping the staircase rail for support, my legs may have buckled beneath me. Instinct had me reaching for the dagger sheathed at my side, but the person I wanted to stab was myself because, surely, I was dreaming. This couldn't be real. Scarlett would never betray me like this, never turn her back on the life we'd built together, and she'd certainly never submit to the goddamn Devil.

I'd almost convinced myself of what I so desperately wanted to believe when she drifted past me; the moment I caught her scent—salty, misty, and so obscenely out of place among all this Navidad bullshit permeating the air—I knew.

This *was* real.

In an instant, I unsheathed my dagger. I saw nothing but red as I raised it, fully prepared to hack and slice just as I'd envisioned no more than an hour ago. Tightening my grip in anticipation of the blood that would soon coat my hands, I took a step forward.

That's when a force slammed me back into the wall with such intensity the wind was knocked from my lungs; before I could catch my breath, a blade slid between my helmet and body armor, the cool steel coming to rest against my throat.

"Put that down before I forget that we're related."

I froze. "Fuck you."

"Put it down, Cedric. I won't ask again."

I'd never hated my phobia of knives more than in that moment. Though my mind protested vehemently, my body obeyed Elvira's words, and she wasted no time snatching the weapon from my quivering fingers.

"This way."

Without removing her dagger from my neck, while the spectators remained distracted, my sister all but dragged me along the wall. Elvira only stopped once we were hidden from view by a nativity tapestry larger than the flags I flew on *The Jolly Serpent* and continued holding me at knifepoint as she spoke in a haggard whisper.

"Listen to me carefully, and do not speak until I'm finished. You do and, I swear to Adais, I will cut you." Inhaling sharply, Elvira pressed her free hand to my shoulder, as if to steady me. "All of this was Scarlett's doing. The chase, your capture, her kidnapping . . . all of it. And everyone knew but you."

My heart thudded wildly even as the rest of me went numb. I wanted to scream, thrash, and wrestle my own sister to the ground if it meant I could continue my bloody rampage, but I didn't do any of that. I just stood there, hollow and empty as I voiced my most pressing thought. "She plotted the death of our *crew*?"

"We lied—Scarlett's orders. They're very much alive."

I stiffened, relieving as the news was. "So all of it was simply to undermine my authority?"

"She didn't betray you," Elvira pressed. "It just had to look that way. If your reactions weren't authentic, if Ruiz didn't buy your act, then this would all fall apart before it began. It's why Scarlett came to me first—"

"When?" I demanded, finally finding my voice. The more Elvira explained, the less this all made sense; she and Scarlett barely tolerated one another and had never *schemed* together—behind my back, no less. "How long have you kn—"

I silenced abruptly when metal nicked my throat. The dagger remained there, its pressure constant and steady.

"May I continue?"

"Yes," I hissed.

"Two months. Adrian got roped into it not long after. Scarlett originally cooked up the idea back when we received word of Jamie's defeat at the hands of Ruiz—when we learned he'd lost everything, including his ship and crew. He barely escaped with his life."

I pieced together what I knew. Jamie was our only surviving brother and the owner of the final medallion shard we needed to obtain. Once we possessed all three, piecing them together would break the curse plaguing me and Scarlett. Simple enough, but this was Jamie Teach we were talking about: the legendary eldest son of Blackbeard, known as the Dragon for his terrifying ferocity. Jamie had two obsessions in life: finding some place called Neverland, where time supposedly stood still, and killing me. Both were equally as insane, though the latter terrified me more than the former. I had long ago accepted the fact that the only way to obtain my brother's shard would be to pry it from his cold, dead hands, for neither of us could live in a world where the other was alive.

But he'd slipped. Our brothers had been close, so when Elvira and I killed Lucas, it shook Jamie to his core. He tried coming after us, but in his haste and sloppiness, got captured by Ruiz instead. Jamie was meant to hang in the square but of course managed to escape; the Dragon wouldn't fall that easily.

"That's *all* he kept, Ced," Elvira continued, interrupting my thoughts and meeting my gaze through the slit in my helmet. "Ruiz took everything else, including Jamie's medallion shard. It's right here within our grasp, and it's what Scarlett risked everything to get. To save you *and* end this game of chase."

"*Save* me?" With rage now overpowering my fear, I shoved against Elvira's chest despite the dagger pressed to my throat. It took every ounce of willpower I still possessed not to scream. "She lied to me. Distrusted me. And look where that got us—we're down to just your shard, now, and we'd still have Lucas's if not for her brilliant plan."

Elvira growled low in her throat. "That particular complication was your doing, brother. None of us thought you'd be foolish enough not to conceal it in the presence of Ruiz. Wasn't 'protect your loot' one of the first things father ever taught us?"

"*Fuck* Blackbeard, and fuck you."

"I understand that this hurts—"

No, she didn't. None of them did. Beyond looking like a complete and utter fool, the pain in my chest was excruciating, and there was no telling whether it was the rot or Scarlett's doing. Did it even matter?

"—and you have every right to be angry. But for Adais's sake, channel that rage into something useful. This isn't the time to lose your head. Clearly, Scarlett can handle herself, so we need to focus on finding the shards. We should split up, gather more information—"

"Split up. Good idea." Another forceful shove loosened Elvira's grip, and I was finally free of that damn knife. Though she reached for me, I darted from her grasp and to the edge of the tapestry where

I dared another peek into the hall. Scarlett and Ruiz's silhouettes were visible, but only just, as they rounded another corner.

I tore off after them.

Most of the crowd had dispersed, but there were still far too many bodies to navigate. The narrow slit in my helmet severely restricted my line of sight, and more than once, I bumped shoulders with one of the many lingering Navy officers. Though they cursed and demanded that I stop and apologize, I didn't, all the while keeping sight of Scarlett's shape.

She and Ruiz weren't alone; a pair of guards each stood at their front and back. I crept as close as I dared, skirting the fine line between arousing suspicion and remaining within earshot.

". . . did well, mi rosa." Ruiz nodded approvingly, his voice a sultry purr. "They're thrilled to see us reunited, England and Spain allies once more."

"As am I." Though I couldn't see Scarlett's face, I heard the smile in her voice, and it summoned a wave of nausea. "These past few weeks have been stifling. It's so freeing not to have to pretend anymore."

Agony pierced my heart. Pretend to do what—love me?

I hardly heard the Admiral's next words, much less comprehended them now that he'd slipped into Spanish. "Solo me puedo imaginar como sería vivír entre ese asqueroso cuervo y su horda de bàrbaros."

Scarlett shot Ruiz a glance. "Inglés, por favor. I told you my Spanish is lacking."

Chills shot down my spine; that was a lie, and a bold one at that. Scarlett was fluent and had been the entire time I'd known her.

What did she have to gain by pretending that she wasn't?

Ruiz sighed as they stopped outside an ornately decorated door. "One of the many things we'll need to remedy."

"Agreed."

My mind was still spinning when right there, in full view of their guards, they kissed. They came together in an instant, and it was far from a quick peck; their mouths parted to allow their tongues access, and their hands roved across one another's bodies to grope places that should only be touched behind closed doors. They fit together perfectly, their movements practiced, and both were as enthusiastic as teenagers who'd discovered sex for the first time.

Tangible bile rose in my throat, and to prevent it spewing from my mouth, I staggered toward the wall, grateful for the Navidad decorations making my concealment easier. Much as I wanted to look away, to gouge my own eyes out, I couldn't. None of this made any sense. There was no way Ruiz didn't know how the curse spread; surely he wouldn't risk being infected by it for the sake of a quick fuck. That left one of two possibilities: either he'd been shielded somehow, or Scarlett had been cured. And once again, I'd been left in the dark.

I raised my gaze. Nothing but red surrounded their writhing bodies as my rage crafted a premonition. I wanted—*needed*—to see them, for it provided an excuse for the blood I was about to spill.

"All of this was Scarlett's doing."

Elvira's words echoed in my head, rattling around until they became hornets. Oh, Scarlett had planned this, all right. She'd twisted the knife of betrayal so deep that I couldn't even grip the handle. Good thing I didn't need it to return the favor.

My bare hands would do.

But as painful as it was, I remained in the shadows, bided my time, and waited. I was confident in my ability to take down one, maybe two men, but Ruiz, Scarlett, and their four guards would be impossible to handle all on my own. If Elvira were here, we might stand a chance as a combined front, but she'd already made it clear she didn't approve of my thirst for revenge. I'd need to do this alone and, to maximize the hurt, remain undetected for as long as possible. My lips twisted into a feral grin, even as Scarlett fondled another man mere meters from me. What would Ruiz do if his staff and guests started dropping like flies, I wondered?

After what felt like an eternity, they broke apart. Ruiz muttered something about duty calling before ushering Scarlett into her room. A pair of guards remained behind while the other two followed Ruiz, and before they had even passed me, I'd decided on my strategy. The moment the guard nearest me glanced the other way, I seized my chance.

He didn't realize I was upon him until my hands were around his throat. Squeezing as hard as I could muster, I waited until his feeble thrashes lessened before giving a sharp, savage twist, snapping his neck. A twinge of discomfort settled in my core as I tossed his lifeless body aside—I'd never once killed a man while his back was turned—but I swallowed it down. If I wanted to win against El Diablo, I couldn't worry about playing fair.

The noise of the body striking the floor was what caught the other guard's attention. Gaze widening through the slit in his helmet, his shaking hands fumbled for the pistol at his belt. "Que eres—"

Should have screamed when you had a chance.

With reflexes to rival Elvira's and fueled by the hunger of my curse, I lunged, aiming for the hand gripping the gun. He anticipated me, but only just; I still managed to wrap my fingers around his wrist. When I twisted at a brutal angle, he cried out. I couldn't have that, so I kept my forward momentum going, slamming his back into the cold stone wall.

Metal rang in both our ears as his helmet screeched from the impact, but instinct kicked in. My attempts to snatch the pistol had thus far failed, and I didn't have a free hand to block the carefully aimed blow to the base of my jaw. It was my turn to grunt as my teeth clipped my tongue, and though I blinked repeatedly, my vision took a few seconds to return—time I couldn't afford.

When at last I glanced up, I stared down the barrel of a gun, and the guard's index finger hovered over the trigger.

"Q-quítate el c-casco," he stammered, trying and failing to hide the terror in his voice. "It's over."

I laughed; it was far from over, but given how I'd killed the other guard, I supposed it was only fair to allow this one to see my face. Careful to avoid touching my throbbing jaw, I removed my helmet, sighing as cool air struck my sweat-coated cheeks.

He gaped. "El pirata?"

"El *Cuervo.*"

With as much force as I could muster, I threw the helmet at his kneecaps. He howled as it found its mark, legs buckling, and I didn't even have to use force to wrestle the gun from his grip. Though he'd hesitated, I didn't.

I shot him between the eyes.

It was quick, but not clean. At such close range, the bullet split his skull, spraying blood across my front before I managed to discard the gun and slip back into the shadows. No doubt, our struggle followed by the gunshot had attracted attention, and sure enough, before his mangled body had ceased its quivering, Scarlett's door burst open.

Stilling, I held my breath as she took in the corpses that were my doing. Only when she knelt to further examine the carnage did I dare to move, creeping silently along the wall containing her door before darting into the room she'd so carelessly left unguarded.

I didn't release the breath I'd been holding until safely concealed within curtains along the far wall, grateful for the cover. My insides were still stitching themselves back together now that I'd killed, and the sensation was so uncomfortable that it took effort to remain silent. But gods, even despite that, this had been easy, *too* easy, but I didn't dare question my luck—not when my goal was within reach. I'd remain here until nightfall or we were alone, whichever came first, and I'd get my answers even if it killed me.

"Lady Maynard," I whispered. "You *really* need better guards."

III. THE CONFRONTATION

Featured Song: A Wayward Storm

My legs had gone numb hours ago, but I refused to move. I'd have refused to breathe if my body hadn't demanded it. I remained silent and still as the grave, even when I'd nearly been discovered during a security sweep of the room. Twice.

I hadn't decided whether Scarlett knew I was there. She had to know I was somewhere within the mansion—who else would have any motive to kill her guards?—but did she know I was *here*, lurking in the one place she should feel the safest? And why would she bother protecting me? Each time I'd been a hair's breadth away from being discovered by those sent to hunt down the mysterious killer, Scarlett had called off the search, citing the need to sweep the grounds yet again. For if the assailant had wormed his way into her quarters, she pointed out, he'd have killed her already. The timing of her interventions felt too convenient to be a coincidence, and yet in the hours since the murders, she hadn't made a single attempt to confront me.

But neither had I. There had been plenty of chances, ample opportunities for us to come head-to-head, but that was just it—I didn't *want* to confront her. I didn't want to know why she'd lied to me, why she'd allowed Ruiz into her bed and, seemingly, her heart. I didn't want to look at the woman I loved and see nothing but an enemy. The Devil and his men could beat me, shoot me, stab me, and it would hurt. I might even bleed.

Scarlett, with mere words, could *ruin* me, and that was agony I simply wasn't prepared for.

We'd been alone for at least an hour, perhaps more. I remained crouched, watching and waiting for . . . something. I hadn't decided what. In the meantime, observing her through a narrow slit in the curtains was nothing short of fascinating. After dismissing her handmaids, she'd slipped into a simple chemise and unbraided her hair. It fell in loose waves down her back, and she made no attempt to brush it. She busied herself with removing her makeup, casting frequent glances into her mirror. All the while, Scarlett hummed to herself. It was a habit I knew well, but I didn't recognize this tune; more than likely it was some Navidad song she'd picked up within these walls. All of it was unmistakably her, her movements, her mannerisms . . . and yet it wasn't.

How had my fiery pirate queen, the woman who had both sailed and commanded the seas by my side, turned into *this* in a matter of days? It was as if Scarlett had become actual royalty, and gods, it suited her just as much as the brutal life she led with me.

Does it? Or have you simply not been paying attention?

I shook my head to clear it of the unpleasant thought just as a winding mechanism caught my attention. Scarlett fiddled with a small object in the corner of her vanity—a music box—turning a key at its base until it began to softly play the very same tune she'd been humming. The notes rang gently and clear, complementing the salty air drifting in from the open balcony. Now that I could hear it better, I realized the song wasn't related to Navidad at all—it was a sailor's lullaby, and an old one at that. Lyrics floated on the breeze, and I became too entranced to care that it wasn't only Scarlett's voice singing them.

"A wayward storm upon the sea,
Star-filled skies are emptied.
Rains are endless, the tide is strong,
They say it won't be long.

Darkness comes to chase the day,
Tattered sails and flags sway.
Howling winds sing a lullaby,
With colors hoisted high.

Twisted paths—who holds the key?
Heave, ho, 'way we go,
Slaves and thieves, all men are freed,
Heave, ho, 'way we go.

Star-touched skin, blood of gold,
As it was foretold.
Chaos reigns in the realm of gods,
But we will beat the odds!

Twisted paths—who holds the key?
Heave, ho, 'way we go,
Slaves and thieves, all men are freed,
Heave, ho, 'way we go."

It didn't end there. Long after the music box had stopped turning, for verses after the lyrics had run out, the melody continued in an endless, haunting loop. I closed my eyes, surrendering both to the music's call and the ethereal voices lingering in midair, but what finally shattered my trance was silence. Scarlett was quick to break that too, her voice laced with venom.

"You can come out now, Cedric."

My blood turned to ice, but I didn't otherwise move as my initial shock turned to rage. How long would she have let me sit there, foolish and agonizing? "You knew I was here this whole time?"

"I've known a lot of things 'this whole time.'" She rose slowly before turning to face me, and I was grateful that the curtains concealed my flinch. I'd never seen the fire in Scarlett's eyes burn as bright as it did now, and it wasn't passion fueling it. It was pure fury, and it matched—maybe even surpassed—my own. "What the fuck are you doing here?"

I burst from the curtains before she'd finished speaking, taking a few steps forward but remaining out of Scarlett's reach. "That's precisely what I came to ask you, but I think I got my answer in that little show you two gave the guards. I did them a favor, killing them— it's something I certainly wish *I* could wipe from my memory."

She laughed darkly. "That's what you're upset about?"

"Among other things."

"I would tell you not to act like a child, but it appears that ship has sailed—"

"—and sunk," I finished flatly. I dared a step closer, but Scarlett anticipated it; we began circling one another like caged wolves. "Having fun playing princess?"

"I'm certainly enjoying the ability to bathe regularly." Her eyes flashed murderously. "Try it—you could wash that blood from your face, and you might find that you like not reeking like a bilge rat on a constant basis."

"You certainly had no problem with *bilge rat* before."

"Neither did you with your *princess*."

We stopped and stared at one another, chests heaving from the force of our insults.

Scarlett regarded me coldly. "If you have something to say,

fucking say it and get it—"

"Why?" My question was only a whisper, but it was enough to shut Scarlett up. I blinked rapidly, fighting to keep the tears I'd summoned in my eyes where they belonged. I was angry, yes, but beneath the hardened surface, I was falling to pieces. "Do I mean so little to you that I wasn't even worth the truth? That you couldn't let me in, trust me with this? *That's* why I'm hurt. I don't care if you're fucking him. I don't even care if you enjoy it. I don't own you—"

That's when she lashed out—with a knife, no less. I didn't know at what point she'd picked it up, nor where she'd plucked it from; all I could concentrate on was the cold steel pressed to my throat. She walked forward, forcing my back against the wall bordering the balcony.

Scarlett's words were sharper than her blade. "No, you don't. Neither does Diego. Neither does *anyone*."

Confusion overtook my fear, but I didn't dare move. Where was she headed with this?

"You're here because you know. You killed those men because you know. But you weren't supposed to, not yet, because I knew you'd act like this. Trust you?" She scoffed against my neck. "I knew you wouldn't trust *me*."

My heart thudded wildly, and not solely because of my phobia. Much as I willed it not to, our proximity summoned desire wildly inappropriate for the present moment, and I had to fight to keep my hands at my sides.

"When we first met, you were my freedom. You were my everything." For the first time tonight, Scarlett was the one to get choked up, but it only lasted a moment before her hardened façade slipped back into place. "I'd known nothing but a life of control—first at the hands of my mother, then the brothel, and finally, my father. No decision I ever made was for myself, not even my engagement to Diego. He promised me a life of luxury, security, and stability, but at the end of the day, I'd just be someone's wife. I couldn't have that. I wouldn't." She met my gaze. "The first thing I ever chose was you."

This time, I had no control over the tear that streaked down my cheek. I'd known as much, of course, but I'd never heard Scarlett say it quite like this. *Haven't you?* that voice within me nagged once more. I swallowed, causing the knife to shift against my neck.

Had she been screaming this entire time, and I simply hadn't been listening?

"I love you, Cedric, and I know you love me. But *gods*, ever since Father's curse spread to us, it's like we don't even speak the same language, and I'm not talking about Spanish. I wasn't your partner anymore. You suddenly saw me as something needing protection, a damsel in distress you needed to keep out of harm's way. Something to control."

I couldn't bring myself to say the words: *I became what you fought so hard to escape.*

Scarlett leaned in; her lips hovered so close to mine that kissing her would be as effortless as taking another breath. "But I am not—I have never been—a fucking damsel. If this doesn't prove it, I don't know what will."

Just like that, she and her knife were gone. I was left a gasping mess, and if not for the wall keeping me upright, no doubt my knees would have buckled. "No . . . damsel," I agreed, finally able to speak. I'd never viewed her precisely that way, but she wasn't wrong about how closely I'd guarded her. Never once had I made certain such an arrangement was what she wanted; I'd acted without thinking. "I was wrong."

"You're damn right you were," Scarlett fired back. She kept hold of the dagger, pointing it in my direction like an accusatory finger. "Retrieving Jamie's shard could have been so painless. I had everything under control, everything planned down to the smallest detail. Diego wrapped around my . . . well, you saw. But then you had to go and do *this*. Two guards, Cedric, really? And as violent as that was . . . You couldn't have pushed one of them out a window and made it look like suicide? That would have made your point just as well." She threw up her hands. "Now, I've got *two* shards to retrieve, Diego up my ass, and the entire mansion on the lookout for you. You won't be able to let down your guard for one second if you want—"

"What can I do to help?" I hadn't wanted to interrupt her, but neither did I want her getting worked up. Most of all, I wanted to set this right. "Tell me and it's done." *Trust me to trust you.*

Scarlett eyed me warily, but after a few moments of silence, lowered the dagger. "The shards aren't easily won. Diego wears both on his person—I told him doing so would protect him from the curse."

I gaped; the shards only protected those they were crafted for. "He's infected, then?"

She nodded. "He'll discover it soon enough, but not until after we've left this place."

Fuck, she truly was cleverer than I'd given her credit for. "Then, how is that not easy? All we need to do is kill him—"

"And how far do you think we'd get, exactly?" Scarlett hissed. "If the lord of this mansion falls, we won't get more than ten feet from this place before we're strung up and hanged—and that's if we're lucky. No matter how much you or I want to, killing him isn't an option."

She had a point, much as I loathed it. "Then, what do we do?"

"Nochebuena." Scarlett's lips played at a smile. "There's a ball that night, and given that it's the eve of our wedding, he and I will be the center of attention. We're expected to dance, to be attached at the hip, and naturally, the shards will be within reach. I intend to procure them the moment he lets his guard down."

"But that's so . . . public." I grimaced as I pictured this going poorly. "Won't he catch you?"

"Perhaps. But he won't *pursue* me—and that's precisely the point of waiting until Nochebuena."

"What do you mean?"

"Diego lives for spectacle," Scarlett pressed. "You saw him parade me through those halls. He has an audience to impress—a massive one at that. Any Naval officer that could be spared is here to celebrate the holiday. Do you seriously think he'd embarrass himself by siccing guards on his runaway bride the eve before his wedding? Before Navidad?" She shook her head. "Diego may order a handful of men after us, but it will be done quietly and nowhere near his full force. Whoever those sorry fools are, we can take them."

And we'd be free—just as she'd promised all along.

"As for what I need you to do? *Survive*. Avoid detection and stay close. I've had to improvise a fair bit given this afternoon, but as soon as I've calmed this down, I'll have orders for you and Elvira. In the meantime, you two are my eyes and ears on the ground—anything of note and I want to hear it."

Scarlett looked at me then, almost as though she expected me to argue, and another tense silence fell. Protest was nowhere near my lips, but there was so much else to say that I didn't know where to start. What a complete and utter fool I'd been? How brilliant she was, how adaptable and conniving? Her unrivaled ability to fool an entire mansion, possibly an entire navy? How sorry I was for underestimating what she could do, and how I'd do whatever it took to make it up to her? How gorgeous she looked, whether by my or Ruiz's side?

Before I could decide or even form a coherent thought, Scarlett had approached me once more. She raised her hand to my face, but this time it didn't contain a knife. Though I willed myself not to move, when she began caressing my cheek, I leaned into her touch.

"You must trust me, Cedric. When this is over, once we survive this, we'll have everything. We'll be *free*."

"I don't want any of it if I don't have you."

The words tumbled out before I could stop them, but I'm not certain I'd have tried. It was the raw, honest-to-gods' truth, and I needed Scarlett to hear it.

She inhaled sharply, shuddering as though I'd stabbed her.

"Look at me."

I met her gaze, unprepared for the intensity swirling in her eyes.

"You may have pissed me off, but you're not getting rid of me that easily." Scarlett smiled softly. "You have me. Now, forever, and always, and we will get through this."

Our kiss tasted as salty as the sea; whether that was because of her tears or mine, I couldn't be certain. Without thinking, I parted my mouth, allowing Scarlett to claim me as I'd claimed her countless times. It felt good, right even, to have her tongue exploring parts of me I couldn't remember ever allowing before, but the urgency of her movements was too much, too fast. I pulled away while keeping hold of her, unwilling to sever our connection completely.

She anticipated my unspoken question, raising her other hand to my cheek. Gripping me gently, her thumb traced the one scar that was her doing. "This isn't *that* kind of goodbye."

"Why does it feel like it?"

"Because you've never surrendered this much control."

Lacking a coherent reply, I simply stared at her. She wasn't referring solely to the kiss we'd just shared; she was talking about this mission, possibly even the entirety of the time I'd known her. Unintentional as it may have been, my efforts to keep her safe and guarded were just as suffocating as the life she'd have led with Ruiz. The life she'd led under her father. Only now did I realize what she'd been trying to tell me all along: a cage is a cage, even if it's shaped like a pirate ship.

"I'm sorry," I whispered.

"I know."

"Allow me to demonstrate," I offered, spreading my arms in surrender, "just *how* sorry. You are a lady, after all—and what Lady Maynard wants, she should very well get."

Scarlett's lips played at a smile. She glanced longingly at the bed; it would be far too easy for us to tumble into it. "I can't say I disagree . . . but you need to go."

"I knew you'd— *What?*"

"I mean it, Cedric. Diego will either send for me, or he'll come here, and you can't be around when he does." Before I could pull her back, Scarlett broke free of our embrace, turning back toward her vanity.

"Can't I just hide?" Panic fluttered in my chest. I'd only just reconciled with her; it truly couldn't be time to abandon her again so soon. "I could eavesdrop, be right here if you need me—"

"If I hadn't been here to protect you, you'd have been caught and hanged already." Scarlett turned, now clutching my discarded helmet. "I covered for you once, but I can promise I won't be able to do it again. Do *not* seek me out unless I send for you myself."

I just stared in silence. I didn't want to argue but wanted to leave her even less.

Scarlett sighed. "What did we establish about trusting me?"

"That I need to."

"Good. Then, you know I mean it when I say we'll see each other later. Get some food and rest, scrub that blood off your face, then join one of the patrols on the grounds. I'll find you once Diego is finished with me."

It took enormous effort not to protest as Scarlett secured my helmet. "And don't take this off again, no matter what happens. If they see your scars, you're dead."

"I know," I muttered.

"Ready?"

I shot her a look, but she thankfully took it as a yes. Leading me to her door, she brought a finger to her lips before opening it just enough to fit her head through.

"¡*Guardia!*" she hissed, panic lacing her voice. "¿Tu habeis oído eso?"

I couldn't make out the garbled Spanish of the men standing outside her door.

"Suena que viene de la sala. ¿Qué esperais? ¡Investigadlo!"

Urgent footsteps reverberated against the stone walls before dying away into nothing.

Scarlett opened the door enough to accommodate me before leaning up to whisper her final piece of encouragement. "We'll get through this."

As I slipped from her chambers and darted down the deserted hall, I forced myself to believe she might be right.

IV. THE BEACH

She wasn't.

For three days, nothing went as we planned. Scarlett never set foot on the grounds that night; as far as I could tell, she hadn't even left her room since our confrontation. As we'd been instructed, Elvira and I gathered plenty of whispers and leads, seized every opportunity afforded to us, did everything we could think of to get a message to Scarlett, but it was no use. We hadn't heard from Adrian, either. Ruiz, without a shadow of a doubt, knew we were here. It was getting increasingly difficult to keep up our ruse, and thanks to the men I'd killed, Scarlett's security had become so tight that I didn't have the slightest idea how she wasn't suffocating. Ruiz rotated out the same handful of guards for her shifts—no doubt his most trusted—so the chances of me being assigned to one were less than zero.

She was still alive; that much I knew. Once I'd figured out where her balcony overlooked the gardens, every night, I got as close as I dared. Even if I only glimpsed her silhouette or shadow, it was enough to ease my pain over being apart for a brief span of time. She'd even stood near the rails once, looking longingly out to sea as that same haunting siren-song echoed in the distance. I knew the feeling well. Coming ashore every now and again was necessary, but that didn't mean either of us were built for it. To be so near you could taste the salt in the air but unable to feel the ocean's caress? That was a special kind of torture, rivaled only by what I felt over the growing distance between us.

Both weighed on my shoulders now. I stood at a grand window overlooking the beach and shuddered when a misty breeze came trickling in, not solely because of the cold. *Trust her.* It should be as easy as breathing, so why was I suffocating? Did I truly think so little of the woman I claimed to love?

I clenched the railing until my knuckles turned white, terrified to know the answer. The sun had set an hour ago, and it was time to head off to meet Elvira, but I couldn't bring myself to move. Doing so would admit defeat, and though it was inevitable, I wasn't ready.

Instead, I fixated upon the way moonlight reflected across the surface of the water. It was a familiar, hypnotizing sight, and for the briefest moment, I felt as though I could breathe. Placing both hands on the windowsill, I leaned forward to inhale even deeper.

That's when movement on the beach caught my eye.

A lone, hooded figure all but glided toward the surf. It was difficult to make out details given the distance and the gathering fog, but when the cloak slipped from the figure's shoulders, the shape became unmistakably female. Other than a chemise so thin it was nearly see-through, she wore nothing else.

My heart skipped a beat, not at her state of dress, but because she kept moving; soon, she'd be in the water. The tide was low, but not necessarily calm, and bound to be so cold it would be like knives piercing her skin. It was one thing to go for a nighttime stroll on the beach, but alone and nearly naked? What in hells was she thinking?

I had to be careful not to startle her. Raising my voice just enough to carry, I kept the panic from my tone. "Miss! Are you all right?" There was no response, so I tried again, louder and more urgently. "Do you need help?"

At this, she turned, and my knees buckled when she smiled.

It was Scarlett.

I couldn't breathe, but apparently, I could run. Instinct and desperation overtook logic, and I sprinted with reckless abandon through the winding mansion halls. Out—I needed to get *out* of here and onto that damned beach. Barreling past the handful of guards who stood in my way, I didn't spare them a second glance nor waste my breath answering their incredulous questions as I descended the stairs two at a time. All the while, that glazed look in Scarlett's eyes haunted me. She wasn't herself. I couldn't explain how I knew, but she hadn't managed to slip past her arsenal of guards simply to catch her breath. She was in danger. And I had to hurry.

After what felt like an eternity, I burst through the lower doors and into the night, discarding my helmet in the sand. There wasn't time to remove my boots and make traversing the beach easier, but I pressed on regardless, frantically scanning the shores for Scarlett. Her cloak remained where she'd tossed it in a crumpled heap, but where had she gone? *No.* Surely, she wouldn't—

There. A relieved sob escaped my lips when a head emerged from the waves, but as I narrowed my gaze, it became clear something wasn't right. The head possessed teeth . . . filed into points.

It opened its mouth, but I covered my ears just in time. I sank to my knees at the pain that seized me, all the while clenching my jaw. Fucking *sirens.* I'd dealt with them before, but as Elvira had pointed out, never this close to human civilization, or even this close to shore. Were they what had lured Scarlett out here? Did their song have hold of her now?

My burning questions were all that gave me the strength to push through the agony of the sirens' cries. Without uncovering my ears, I used my teeth to rip the collar of my shirt into a long strip. I stuffed one ear and then the other, ignoring the blood trailing from my lobes and the pounding in my skull as I struggled to my feet. The makeshift stuffing wouldn't shield me from the pain but should be enough to prevent me from losing my agency to the siren's whims, at least for the time being.

I raised my chin at the awful creature, speaking though I couldn't hear my own voice. "You'll have to try harder than that."

With a hiss, the siren slipped below the surface of the waves once more, but I didn't dare remove the stuffing; where there was one siren, there were more. A gentle hum rattled my bones, and I knew then it was the very thing that had Scarlett under its spell. Contrary to some of the myths, siren-song affected both sexes equally, and I hadn't noticed any protection covering her ears. She'd disappeared from the endless expanse of beach in both directions, and that meant only one thing.

They'd dragged her under.

The chilling realization had me removing my excess clothing: the uniform, my boots, all of it, until all I wore were my undershirt and trousers—the equivalent to Scarlett's chemise. Staggering toward the waves, I only allowed myself a single steady breath before entering the tide.

Cold. It was just as painful as I'd imagined, and maybe even worse because I hadn't properly braced myself. Numbness shot up my legs and settled in my core, where instinct screamed for me to turn back. I did the opposite; the moment the water reached my torso, I dove forward to submerge my entire body beneath the surface of the tide.

Agony replaced mere discomfort, and despite being underwater, I stifled a curse. Though my frozen limbs protested vehemently, I swam forward and down at a slight angle. Opening my eyes took effort, and it was just as I expected—darkness. But I didn't need to see. It was that low hum guiding me, each pulse of the siren's song causing the hair on my arms to stand at attention. Just a little farther, and—

Saltwater flooded my lungs as I opened my mouth in a silent scream. Something sharp pierced my ankle and then my opposite shoulder, twisting and digging as teeth sharp as daggers attempted to tear flesh from bone. Though I thrashed and kicked, I couldn't shake the sirens latched onto me, and the energy I wasted doing so was rapidly eating up any oxygen I had to spare. Their cruel laughter echoed in my ears, as did their awful tongue, the language harsh and abrasive even when spoken underwater.

I gritted my teeth, my agony turned to fury. These monsters could do whatever they liked to me, but I wasn't surfacing without Scarlett. *Where is she?* Though my eyes remained open, all I saw were flashes of the sirens' golden scales glittering in the moonlight as more swam around me, prepared to feast on whatever was left as soon as their companions were finished. A frenzy gathered below, lying in wait like a den of gilded sharks. They began calmly but grew more agitated the more my blood clouded the water, while I grew weaker as my strength—and breath—left me.

Air. That became my central thought; I needed to surface, and soon. The pain in my limbs hardly compared to the agony in my lungs, and I was no longer fighting to be free. I was fighting to breathe. To *live.* Effort turned to panic, but even pure survival instinct could only get me so far.

It was over quickly. There were too many of them, and I had no strength left to fight. The cold had crept into my bones, and there was no escaping the chill that encompassed me now. Numbness settled in my core, followed by a strange warmth, and I turned my face toward it, welcoming death.

Still. Silent and still.

But then . . . movement. Arms wrapped around my middle at the same moment the sirens released me. I became vaguely aware I was rising, floating, though whether it was to the surface or beyond, I couldn't be certain and didn't care. I didn't feel much of anything until frigid wind struck my cheek, but my airway was far too blocked to draw a decent breath—any breath. My barely conscious, violently shaking form allowed itself to be dragged up the beach, only just out of reach of the waves. There I lay lifelessly, helpless until a force pounded on my chest.

"*Breathe*, goddammit!"

I sputtered, choking on the nauseating mixture of spittle and seawater that spewed from my throat, but remained unable to do as the voice commanded.

"Stay with me—that's an order."

Another strike, this one landing squarely on my sternum. I didn't have a chance to choke; all I could do was roll on my side and retch as fluid poured freely onto the sand. The desperate, horrendous need to draw a heaving breath soon followed, but there wasn't time for that, either. I became pinned on my back by that same relentless force, and before I could protest, I'd been straddled.

"Shit, what did they do to you? Why are you *here*?"

My lips moved, but they couldn't form words. I was breathing now despite the weight on my lower body—a comforting weight despite the pain from my wounds. There was something intimately familiar about the way the presence moved and spoke, but I didn't recognize her beyond a doubt until she kissed me.

Scarlett tasted of blood and salt. Her mouth covered mine while her hands moved to my face, but I caught both before she could do whatever it was she intended. An overwhelming desire to touch her, to combine our bodies to combat the chill became all-encompassing. Ignoring the blood—my blood—flowing freely onto the sand, I pushed against her to pull myself upright, all the while keeping my lips pressed to hers. Gods, it felt right, I was complete for the first time in—

A sharp pain to my temple caught me off guard. I staggered back, stumbling into the rolling tide as it receded around my wounded shoulder. Ignoring the sting, I looked up to find Scarlett towering over me, soaking wet and furious. She quivered, though I wasn't certain whether it was from the cold or her rage. Perhaps both.

"What the fuck, Cedric?" she hissed through chattering teeth.

I lifted my hand to my throbbing skull, inhaling sharply at the simple brush of my fingertips. "Did you . . . hit me?"

"I was resuscitating you, not kissing you—"

"Both were fine by me."

"You absolute *ass*." If it were anyone but Scarlett glaring at me like that, I may have been genuinely terrified. Her gaze flicked to my bites and back again, almost as if she didn't want to acknowledge the existence of my wounds. "I had everything under control."

"Like fuck you didn't!" My injured leg was of little concern as I leaped to my feet, raising my voice along with my body. Though I remained freezing, the icy sensations became secondary to my rage. "I believed you once, but that excuse won't fly a second time. What in the gods' names were you doing out here? You had to know about the sirens; I've heard them all week—"

"You have?" Her demeanor changed in an instant, fury melting into genuine surprise. "How?"

"What do you mean, *how*? I know what sirens sound like." I couldn't make out their song now, thank Adais; my ear stuffing had fallen out in the water. Had they gotten their fill of my flesh, or had Scarlett fought them off somehow?

"You weren't supposed to hear," Scarlett muttered so quietly I almost didn't make out her words. But when she raised her chin, both her inner fire and irritation returned with a vengeance. "You aren't supposed to *be* here. I haven't sent for you, haven't needed you—"

"What would you have me do, sit and twiddle my thumbs while you jump into a freezing cold sea at the behest of sirens? How is that not needing me?"

Scarlett crossed her arms, shuddering as the wind kicked up. "In case you haven't noticed, I saved *your* ass—not the other way around."

"But how?" I pressed. She bristled, but I cut across her. "The question doesn't have the slightest bit to do with my pride. You saved my life, I'm grateful, but *how*? I'd have been eaten alive, and I went in *after* you. How is it that you not only pulled me out, but there's also not a scratch on you?"

"I'm the stronger swimmer; I dodged them—"

"Bullshit," I snapped. "I saw that look in your eyes. The sirens had you under their spell. Unless . . . they didn't?"

Scarlett simply stared at me, and that was enough for my mind to begin sprinting to wild conclusions. She wasn't hurt. She wasn't freezing—at least as far as I could tell—*and* she had been strong enough to save me from a horde of bloodthirsty sea creatures. There was only one answer that made any logical sense, so to test whether she would argue, I stated it as fact.

"You had a reason for coming out here. I want to know what it was."

She raised her chin. "I've asked you time and time again to trust me. Is that not enough?"

"It's not." I took a step toward her, and she didn't back away. "Scarlett, I want the truth. I *have* trusted you; I've kept quiet, done as you asked. But there's something you're not telling me, something big, and it's high time I learned what that is. I can step into the dark. I can follow you blindly. I would kill—I have killed—for you. But how can I leap off a cliff if I don't know you're at the bottom to catch me?"

At this, she fell silent. Her lips quivered, but it remained impossible to tell whether emotion or the cold was its cause. Water dripped rhythmically from her sopping-wet hair into the sand, matching the blood still trickling from my wounds.

"You're hurt," Scarlett forced out, breaking the silence. Neither of us moved; we were both as unwilling to close the remaining distance between us as we were to back away.

I responded with the only thing I could manage, fully aware she hadn't answered my question. "Yes." Flesh wounds. Provided the siren bites didn't get infected, I'd heal and would be left with even more scars to add to my ever-growing collection. They used to bother me, but not anymore; the marks were as part of me as the rest of my past.

"You need to get those looked at."

"Elvira can stitch me up."

Scarlett raised a brow. "I meant by a *real* medic."

"And explain what bit me?" I laughed darkly. "No thanks."

"I won't lose you over an untreated wound—"

"I won't lose you over *this*." We were inches apart now, but at what point that had happened, I wasn't certain. "Why can't you just tell me the truth? We're partners, and a week ago we were inseparable, we were ..."

My voice trailed off at the realization that Scarlett's lips hovered dangerously close to mine in an unspoken question. She whispered against them but remained at a calculated distance. "The truth is that I'm terrified of losing you."

It would have been so easy to kiss her. I badly wanted to. But her words made me grasp her chin instead, and I lifted it to look her in the eye. "I'm right here."

"Then prove it."

At such a bold invitation, my little remaining self-control melted away, as did any lingering pain. Weaving my fingers through her tangled hair, I used my free hand to grip Scarlett's hip, pulling her lower body against my own. She moaned into my mouth as I claimed her. Her hands roamed my chest, tracing muscle and scars alike before settling on my uninjured shoulder and cheek, nails digging into my skin just enough to spur me on. Our tongues moved in rhythm, and our bodies writhed as one as we danced to music only we could hear.

Heat was everywhere, but most of it settled in my core—and below. It hadn't taken long at all for my cock to harden, not with the way Scarlett moved, and a week of pent-up frustration could no longer be contained. With both of my arms around her, I used one of my legs to kick hers out from beneath her before lowering us onto the sand. We remained within reach of the tide, but neither of us cared, even as a wave enveloped Scarlett's lower half. She arched her back as I moved my lips to her neck and wasn't shy about gripping the back of my head to guide me where she wanted. I resisted, only to nuzzle her breasts as she pulled me lower, and lower still, until my elbows rested on either side of her hips and my chin hovered between her legs.

Her chemise had bunched up, the white blending in with the foam of the tide. The wet fabric hugged her gorgeous shape and didn't leave much to the imagination, but I wanted to see her—all of her. With Scarlett's help, I untangled the skirt from her legs, not stopping until her lower half had been fully exposed. She shuddered as wind caressed her bare thighs; jealous of even the elements giving her the same pleasure I intended to, I quickly moved in. Gripping the undersides of her legs, I began at her left knee, trailing my lips downward in a series of urgent kisses.

I waited until she'd propped herself up on her arms and was able to meet my gaze before kissing her *there*.

Scarlett responded immediately, throwing her head back and gasping as I moved my tongue in what I knew were agonizing strokes. I relished the taste of her but forced myself to go slow, wanting to draw out her pleasure for as long as possible. Her thighs pressed against either side of my head, both trapping me exactly where I would have been happy to remain forever and informing me she felt the same. This moment was about her, but beyond that, it was an apology. I'd fucked up for reasons far beyond those I'd originally thought back in the prison and didn't intend to squander my one chance to make it up to her.

Only once I'd gotten her thoroughly warmed up in more ways than one did I move to more sensitive areas. Scarlett's squirming made it difficult, but I remained slow and steady as I traced circles around the tiny bud already standing at attention. The sight sent a wave of pleasure down to my groin, and I moaned against her entrance as my cock stiffened against my pants. I gripped her thighs tighter, spreading her, and dared a single flick at the elusive bud. She cried out, more agonized over the fact that I didn't linger there than the flick itself.

"Cedric." Gods, the way Scarlett said my name sent shivers down my spine. "Please, fuck me. I want you to."

"Not yet." At least, not in the way she meant. I had other ideas for right now—ones I knew she'd be amicable to if only she would lie still. I went back to doing longer strokes, ignoring her gentle but insistent pulling of my hair. "Touch yourself if you can't stand it."

She didn't need to be told twice. Scarlett's hands moved to her own breasts, and though I didn't want to stop what I was doing, I couldn't help but lift my eyes to watch. She kneaded and squeezed, thumbs working her nipples while her gaze remained locked on mine. With her mouth slightly parted, cheeks flushed, and her hair and clothing in disarray, I'd never seen anything half as beautiful.

It got me going like nothing that had come before, and I decided I couldn't stand making either of us wait any longer. With passionate urgency, I parted her folds with one hand before plunging my tongue inside her, keeping hold of Scarlett even as her hips bucked against me. She cursed into the night, her cry swallowed by the roll of the tide as I used both my fingers and mouth to pleasure her in tandem, taking turns sucking, licking, and fucking her all at once. I watched her body closely, my own arousal growing as her legs clenched around me, the pleasure consuming her in waves.

When Scarlett climaxed, I nearly did, too. I kept my fingers inside her as she twitched and writhed and didn't cease the movements of my tongue until she had squeezed the orgasm for all it was worth. Only once she was breathless and still did I pull away and push myself into a sitting position, but only to reposition myself on top of her. My cock remained hard, not at all helped by the fact that it now pressed against the area I'd worked so hard to pleasure, but if Scarlett was sensitive, she didn't show it. She welcomed my kiss with enthusiasm, tangling her fingers in my hair and forcing my body even closer to hers.

Only once she had licked nearly every trace of her orgasm from my lips did I break our kiss. As she worked to catch her breath, I brushed a few strands of hair from her face, smiling at the glow that lit her cheeks. "You're gorgeous when you're satisfied."

Scarlett frowned. "Who said anything about satisfied? Do I

look finished?"

Before I could respond, she used a form of the same tactic I'd utilized earlier to pull herself out from under me. Taking advantage of the momentum, she reversed our positions, and a moment later, I was the one pinned in the sand with the rolling tide at my back.

"I'm far from finished, Cedric Teach. But first, you have to close your eyes."

A week ago, I may have argued, but tonight I didn't dare. Resisting the urge to grip Scarlett's hips and keep that tantalizing weight atop my groin, I didn't move even when she rose from her position.

"Are you looking?"

I barely suppressed a grin; temptress was evidently her chosen role. "No."

"Good."

The tide was so loud it was impossible to make out her footsteps even as she padded along wet sand. I had no idea in which direction she'd gone, nor what for, but had no doubt the wait would be worth it. Scarlett hadn't admitted it aloud, but I knew already that I'd just given her some of the most intense pleasure of her life. If she intended to reciprocate, what could she possibly have in store for me? Shivers shot up my spine as my mind raced with a plethora of possibilities.

I wasn't certain how long I lay there, eyes closed and limbs splayed, but it was more than a few minutes. There remained no trace of Scarlett, no trace of anyone or anything other than the faint siren-song carried on the breeze. I didn't dare peek but raised my voice the slightest bit. "Scarlett? Are you—"

"She is. But unfortunately for you, not alone."

The voice that had spoken was the very last I'd expected to hear. Twisting and scrambling, I only managed to get on all fours before stronger arms than mine yanked and pinned my wrists behind my back. They were secured with shackles icier than the frigid sea. A harsh blow landed on the back of my knees, forcing me into a kneeling position and summoning a groan from my lips, and just like that, I was a prisoner again.

Blinking in disbelief, I took in the sight before me. A dozen guards with Ruiz at their head—all gloved so as not to touch my cursed skin directly—may have been of concern if it weren't for the mess of still-wet hair hiding among them. She'd donned a Navy jacket and kept her gaze trained to the sand, but it was unmistakably Scarlett. No restraints of any kind held her in place, and when she finally lifted her eyes to mine, I flinched at the pure loathing I saw within—in stark contrast to how she'd looked at me not even half an hour ago.

My blood ran cold, pulse spiking as I stared at her. The glow of sex had left her, as had any traces of light, leaving behind nothing but a hardened, cruel shell. Had Scarlett left my side only to summon Ruiz and his men? Her now-chilling admission echoed in my mind: "*The truth is that I'm terrified of losing you.*" Had this been her intention all along, to slip away the moment I was good and distracted? Had the woman I loved betrayed me—right after she let me fuck her? Used me like I was nothing?

Was that all I was to her now?

The rest of the crowd melted away; I spoke only to her, voice raw and hoarse. "I don't understand. What are you—"

"Cállate," the man behind me growled. Gloved hands yanked my hair so roughly it summoned tears to my eyes, forcing my head in Ruiz's direction. "Dirígete al Almirante o no hableis en lo absoluto."

"He doesn't understand much Spanish," Scarlett butted in, shoving her way to stand beside Ruiz.

"He understands *this* just fine."

I barely registered Ruiz's words before the admiral landed a savage kick to my ribcage. I doubled over, suppressing my groan yet welcoming the physical pain. At least it hurt far less than Scarlett's treachery. He lashed out a second time once I was down, this time connecting with my chin. My jaw snapped shut, clipping my tongue in the process, and when the guard once again yanked my hair to pull my head back, blood trailed down my split lip.

Ruiz knelt to my level. His gaze lingered on my numerous wounds and bruises, and he flashed me a cruel smile. "Well, it seems as though El Cuervo won't be flying away this time. Have we thoroughly clipped your wings, Crow?"

I should have kept silent. I should have remained still. But I had nothing left to lose and refused to go down without one final twist of the only knife I was capable of wielding. "They won't save you, you know."

He frowned. "What?"

"Those." My gaze flickered to the medallion shards glittering on his chest: one embossed with a dragon, the other a wolf. "The shards only protect those they were crafted f—"

Pain exploded across my already sore temple as another blow landed there, cutting me off mid-sentence. Spots danced in my vision, but when it finally came back, I made out Scarlett standing over me, hand still raised; she'd hit me a second time.

She continued glaring daggers as she curled her lip in disgust. "Get him out of my sight."

Ruiz stood, taking Scarlett's hand and kissing it. "Of course, mi rosa. We have a wedding to plan."

The wedding. I'd nearly forgotten tomorrow was Nochebuena and the day after that, Navidad. I'd not simply failed, it was over; by this time tomorrow, Scarlett would be dancing with the devil, and by the next, she would be his wife.

But what about the shards—Scarlett's carefully-laid plan? What about Elvira? Adrian? Did *he* know any of this, and where the hell was he? Why hadn't he come for us? My mind spun as I was dragged to my feet, and the more I tried to piece everything together, the less it all made sense. One thing remained an irritating constant, though: Scarlett's insistence upon me trusting her. The optimistic part of me wanted to do nothing more, but the realistic part had already plunged into a deep, terrifying darkness, not at all helped by the chains currently binding my wrists. I gritted my teeth as I watched her walk away hand in hand with Ruiz. Rage boiled beneath my skin, contained only by the fact that I was restrained. Trust her? After *this*?

I'd sooner fucking kill her.

V. THE BALL

Admiral Ruiz's grand hall looked straight out of a fairy tale. I didn't have the slightest idea how he'd managed it, but the indoor space had been transformed into a picturesque winter landscape, complete with falling snow. White blanketed the floor and gathered on every available surface, including the massive conifers which served as centerpieces, but never once threatened to put out the dozens of candles and lanterns serving as illumination. It puzzled me. The snow wasn't cold, yet it was in no danger of melting and didn't seem to hinder the maids and servants as they bustled about without a second glance, nor the orchestra musicians tuning and warming up. Wreaths and ornaments hung everywhere, adding color to the otherwise too-bright space, and the hall smelled of cinnamon and pine. It wasn't simply decorated for Nochebuena; it was as if Navidad itself had vomited and spewed, leaving no corner untouched.

I swallowed, forcing down the bile that had risen in my own throat. If anyone had told me even a day ago that I'd be here to witness such a marvel, I'd have keeled over laughing; now, all I wanted to do was cry, especially with the wedding arbor staring me down. It was made up of intricately woven branches, covered in frost, and woven with delicate blue ribbon. A bell hung from the top, ready and waiting to be rung. It was the physical manifestation of a singular truth I had yet to acknowledge—one I wasn't certain I even could.

Scarlett and Ruiz's union would take place tonight.

Pain blossomed in my chest, and it wasn't my curse. Though I'd already done so countless times, I tested the manacles that kept me fastened to the table and chair serving as my current prison, inhaling through gritted teeth as my injuries smarted from the movement. Last night had been one of the most uncomfortable nights of my life, but I'd much rather have remained strung up in that stinking dungeon covered in my own filth than dragged out here. My wounds had been dressed enough to keep me from bleeding all over Ruiz's pristine floor, and I'd been bathed to keep from offending his esteemed guests. Most had yet to arrive, but a few had begun trickling in, shooting me puzzled glances and muttering as if I couldn't understand every word—the words spoken in English, that is. My mind was far too addled to bother with Spanish, and as far as I was concerned, they could call me whatever they liked.

No one was coming to save me; that much was crystal clear. I hadn't seen Elvira since before my capture, and Adrian's whereabouts remained a mystery. My men were apparently alive, but I hadn't heard nor seen any trace of them for nearly a week, and for all I knew, they didn't give two shits about my current predicament and would sooner let me rot . . . literally. If Ruiz didn't plan on killing me tonight, I had no doubt he'd simply let my curse do the rest. I had no weapons, no plan, and no allies, and all I could do was sit and watch this nightmare unfold.

The hall was soon filled nearly to the brim. Ruiz's guests were predominantly naval officers and their crews. Though it was difficult to make out details now that the sun had set, the window to my left had a rather magnificent view of the harbor. An armada of Spanish ships lay idle, docked and sparsely guarded, while everyone else enjoyed the holiday. There was drinking and dancing to be had, and though a few couples weaved and whirled around the floor, there remained an open space in the middle.

I tried not to stare, but it was as though my eyes were glued to the spot. Scarlett's words echoed in my head—*we're expected to dance, to be attached at the hip*—and though they hadn't yet appeared, all I could picture were her and Ruiz doing just that, except attached in . . . . other places. My first glimpse of them, their kiss in the hall, the way they'd acted as a team just last night—all of it replayed in my mind up until the moment they really did appear.

Cheering and applause broke the monotonous chatter, and the crowd parted without prompting. Hand in hand, Ruiz and Scarlett entered the grand hall; my gaze shifted to the pair of medallion shards resting on the admiral's chest before flickering back to the pair. Though Ruiz looked nothing short of magnificent in his formal coat and dress, she looked straight out of a dream.

Scarlett's gown was pure white adorned with gold trimmings. The decoration ended at her waist where the material flowed into a seemingly endless, sweeping skirt, its color blending perfectly into the snow. Her train was so long she had a maid carrying it, and in her free hand, she clutched a dozen perfectly manicured roses. A veil covered her face, but despite the barrier, I swore our gazes met.

Before I could mouth something, Ruiz's sudden declaration had me flinching at its volume. "Ladies and gentlemen, my dear guests, allow me to formally welcome you to our Nochebuena ball. As some of you may have heard, this event doubles as a special occasion: tonight, Lady Scarlett will do me the immense honor of becoming my wife."

Had there been any food in my stomach, I would have retched it up right then and there.

"But first, *bailamos*."

Either it all happened quickly, or my mind simply refused to process the goings-on, but before I knew it, Scarlett and Ruiz were whirling about the floor in an elaborate, complicated waltz. Her train was evidently just an extra-long cloak so had been easily shed, but Scarlett's veil remained in place as they danced. The orchestra itself seemed barely able to keep up with the pair as they flew, and I gaped, unable to fathom how it was the Scarlett I knew moving like that.

Then again, I'd been unable to process how she could be doing any of this to me. I'd followed her instruction exactly, placed my faith in her, *surrendered* to her, and the only place it had gotten me was in chains. Perhaps this had been her plan all along—revenge, but not against Ruiz. Against *me* for suffocating her and holding her captive when all she'd sought was freedom, with the endgame being to force me to watch this ceremony.

But that's where logic ended because how was being married to the Devil any better? I wasn't perfect, but neither was Ruiz, and trapped within these walls seemed a far worse fate than sailing the open sea. How could she stand to be that close to him, touch him like—

"Don't move."

The whisper was so slight I barely heard it; I might have believed I was hearing things had a presence not enveloped me from behind. "Elvira?"

"That's moving— Shut the fuck up."

Stilling, I barely breathed as my sister ducked below the table. The iron around my ankles shifted as she inserted a key into one and then the other, but when I tried to pull my leg away, she firmly yanked it back into place.

"What part of 'sit still' don't you understand?" she hissed. "It needs to look as though you're still restrained."

Why? I barely swallowed the question burning in my throat. Elvira clearly intended to get me out, but what about Scarlett? Was she in on whatever my sister had planned, or was I about to leave her behind for good?

Unlocking my wrists went much slower and took careful stealth.

Elvira could only move when she was certain no eyes were on us, and even then, she only dared to perform miniscule movements at a time. Remaining silent through it all was torture, and more than once, I bit my tongue to keep from voicing my racing thoughts aloud.

Only once I was fully freed did Elvira offer an explanation. "Stay right here and do not let anyone see what I did, but be ready to *move*, and move quickly."

"When?" I dared to ask.

"You'll know," was all my sister offered before darting away. Her sudden absence bothered me more than I cared to admit, as did the fact that Ruiz and Scarlett's waltz was ending. Much as I loathed watching it, I'd rather them dance forever than sit through what came next.

Their wedding.

The couple made their way to the wedding arbor, but I was too busy deciding which bothered me more: the fact that my brothers' shards hung around Ruiz's neck or that Scarlett had done nothing to retrieve them. Not wanting to risk shifting my loose shackles by clenching my fists, I gritted my teeth instead. How could she possibly resist snatching them when they were *right there*?

"Lady Scarlett, if you could remove your veil."

My head snapped up. Were they skipping steps, or had I really been so lost in thought that I'd missed half the ceremony?

"Allow me," said Ruiz, and a moment later, Scarlett's face emerged, but she wasn't looking at him.

She was looking at me.

Ignoring the gasps of shock, she picked up her heavy skirt to take a few steps in my direction. Brows knotted in concern and her voice laced with urgency, Scarlett bellowed a single word. "*DUCK!*"

My body moved before my mind caught up, diving beneath the table a moment before glass rained down around me. The floor shuddered around the same time, the entire mansion groaning as it worked to withstand whatever had just struck it, but I didn't hear much after that. Static ringing replaced what I was certain were screams of terror mixed in with the destruction; I may have joined them had dusty debris not flooded my mouth.

Blinking the tears from my eyes, I remained beneath the table but dared a peek in the harbor's direction. The window had shattered, leaving behind nothing but a bent and broken frame and revealing a clear view of what was happening below. Though my hearing hadn't fully returned, I made out the faint *boom* of cannon fire, coupled with what I swore was more siren song—but that was of little concern compared to the harbor itself.

Broadside and mercilessly firing upon the helpless armada was *my ship*. Fuses and their explosions lit the night, as did the flames from the naval ships already burning. *The Jolly Serpent's* colors flapped proudly in the breeze, and there, gripping the rail, was a man distinctly Adrian's shape—

"—doing? Get *away* from there!"

Something yanked me farther back just as another shuddering blow sent those still standing toppling. The mansion quivered from floor to ceiling, moving as if an earthquake rippled beneath us.

Decorations toppled, guests screamed and crowded the doorways, and what I had once called a fairy tale had instantaneously transformed into a nightmare.

"Ced, we need to move—"

"Scarlett." I shrugged off Elvira's grip as I scanned the chaos for her, unwilling to leave her behind. "Where is she?"

"Taking care of herself, I'm sure." Elvira pulled on my arm once more. "We need to get out of here before this place collapses!"

"You go. I won't be long."

My sister's curse became lost among the chaos as I left her to run straight into the thick of the rubble. Beyond a sea of broken glass, it was damn near apocalyptic—an entire wall had toppled, crushing dozens in the process. The more I took in, the clearer it became that the window hadn't shattered of its own accord; a *cannon* had been fired at it, evidenced by the destruction I'd witnessed many times before.

But where was Scarlett? Ruiz? I screamed her name until I couldn't any longer, unsure if I was even heard over the clamor that continued around me. The floor twitched and shook violently now; surely, it wouldn't be long until, as Elvira had predicted, this entire place came down around us. Beneath the screams of terror, there were groans of pain as the wounded begged to be helped, and the clouds of dust were becoming so thick it was impossible to see—

"Maldita perra," a hoarse voice spat, turning my blood to ice. There, half-buried in rubble, was Ruiz. Standing over him was Scarlett, a dagger held to his unflinching throat.

"At least I'm not a fool." Snatching both medallion shards between her fists, she yanked, snapping the cords before shooting him a smug grin. "And by the way, Cedric was right. You *are* cursed."

He opened his mouth to speak but silenced when Scarlett pressed her dagger into his flesh just enough to summon blood.

"Enjoy your stay in hell, El Diablo—"

"Scarlett."

I shouldn't have interrupted—I badly wanted to let her continue—but the walls were shaking, and there was no time to waste. She blinked before nodding, dropping her knife at Ruiz's chest.

"Here—maybe this will save you from needing to chew yourself out."

"Are you two done playing theater?" hissed a voice from behind. I turned to see Elvira emerge from a cloud of dust, more serious than I'd ever seen her. "The servants' pathways. Now!"

She led the way to a door I wouldn't have located on my own, and with Scarlett's help, we managed to yank it open. The stairs it revealed were intact and clear, and I kept hold of both Elvira and Scarlett as we descended them, leaving the screams and devastation behind.

A few more twists and turns and evasion of the crowd, and we soon found ourselves on the mansion's beach. Though the women took off in the opposite direction nearly right away, I stopped to stare openmouthed at the destruction *The Jolly Serpent* had caused; the burning, the ruin, the carnage. An armada of capable ships had been reduced to rubble, and though it saddened me to see such vessels go to waste, each of them felled would be one less with which to come after us. Not that Ruiz would dare, given his humiliation—

"Cedric, are you coming?"

I turned to see Scarlett waiting for me. She held the medallions in one hand and extended her other, but I found myself shaking my head in disbelief. "What happened? Did you . . . ?"

"Plan this? Yes." She gestured for me to come along. "And I'll explain everything later, I promise, but right now we need to go."

"Where?" I glanced again at the harbor, at *The Jolly Serpent*; surely, we weren't leaving it behind?

Though I wasn't looking at her, I heard the smile in Scarlett's voice. "Home."

VI. THE FAIRY

The only thing keeping me the slightest bit warm was the drink in my hand; despite two shirts, a scarf, and the thickest jacket I owned, it took effort to keep my teeth from chattering. Icy winds battered both me and *The Jolly Serpent* relentlessly, causing the sea to toss and turn below us. This time of year was less-than-ideal for sailing, and it was an even worse idea to be gathered out on deck like we were—the weather could turn into a storm at any given moment—but no man had wanted to remain safe and warm below. The elements may have been against us, but the festivities wouldn't stop even if I ordered them to. Not when there was both a victory *and* a holiday to celebrate. Laughter cut through the chill, and there was drinking, music, and dancing to be enjoyed. A few of the men had even exchanged gifts, and someone had hung mistletoe from one of the railings.

I'd never witnessed a more perfect night, and thanks to Elvira and Adrian, it was a night I could enjoy. My sister guarded all three medallion shards well out of reach of the drunken partygoers, and though Adrian was present, he refused to partake in the celebration, remaining alert to our surroundings. I seriously doubted such precautions were necessary but didn't dare refuse the opportunity to let my guard down—not when it meant I could study Scarlett from afar.

Though my men were doing a fine job of celebrating, there was no doubt she was the most joyful of them all. Though she remained careful not to touch anyone skin-to-skin, Scarlett had taken turns dancing with any man who would have her, and her smile was as infectious as her laugh. It even had the corners of my own mouth twitching right up until the moment she halted in front of me.

"Come dance!"

I nearly choked on my rum. Once I'd placed it on the barrel beside me, I raised my skeptical gaze to hers. "Haven't you had enough of that for at least a little while?"

"For Adais's sake, it's Navidad." Her eyes twinkled. "And I know you haven't gotten me a present—"

"I was a bit busy keeping my head on my shoulders!"

"—so let mine be this." Scarlett turned deadly serious as she removed her gloves and extended her hand, and my stomach dropped at the sight. She'd shed her wedding dress for her typical disorganized garb: one of my old shirts, a Navy jacket she'd stolen off an officer, men's breeches, and boots laced up to her knees. Her dark hair tumbled loosely about her shoulders, and a pistol rested at her hip. This was the Scarlett I knew and loved, and now that she was back, I didn't intend to let her go. I slipped my hand into hers. Her grip was firm and sure, steadying me in more ways than one as she pulled me to my feet, and before I knew it, we were gliding across *The Jolly Serpent's* slippery, frigid deck.

"See, this isn't so bad."

I grimaced. "Maybe not for you." Scarlett was the one leading our dance while I did my best to simply keep up.

She snorted. "Don't pretend that I could make the great Cedric Teach, son of Blackbeard, do a single thing he didn't want to."

"For you, I'd do anything."

Scarlett grinned before resuming leading us in what was turning out to be an impressive display despite my awkwardness. Fiddle, hurdy gurdy, and accordion took turns cranking out the melody of a modified waltz, and before I knew how, Scarlett and I were flying. The longer we danced, the easier it became to anticipate her movements. Weaving and turning as only true partners could, we utilized the entirety of available space, crowding out men dancing with their own lovers. We only stopped once the musicians played their final note.

Breathless and giggling, Scarlett threw her arms around me. When her lips found mine, I reciprocated eagerly, gripping the side of her neck to pull her closer. It wasn't close enough, so my hands traveled even lower, lingering on her hips and ass—

"Plenty of time for that," Scarlett managed with a smirk, pulling herself just out of reach. "Walk with me?"

I nodded after a quick glance around. There was no sign of Elvira, so she must have still been with the shards, and Adrian nodded when I met his gaze, informing me he'd keep his watch. It left me free to follow Scarlett, but she didn't head belowdecks as I expected. She wandered to the upper deck, stopping to lean on the railing as she observed the goings-on from above.

I positioned myself behind her, snaking my arms around her middle and leaning my chin on her shoulder. We remained like that for several minutes, weaving aimlessly to the music; she traced the scars on my wrists while I took several deep inhales of her hair. Scarlett's scent flooded me with warmth and something else as I recalled the last time we had been this close. Golden scales flashed in my mind, their color accentuated by the moonlight as they slipped silently below the waves.

"Is it true that you can talk to sirens?"

The question slipped out before I could stop it, but Scarlett didn't react other than to turn her head slightly. "It's not . . . talking, exactly. But I can understand them, and they seem to understand me."

"And that's how Adrian knew to come for us?" He'd told me as much once I'd boarded *The Jolly Serpent* following our escape, but if I was honest, I still didn't quite believe it. When had Scarlett developed such an ability, and how? "Can Adrian understand them, too?"

Scarlett chuckled. "It's not as difficult as you might think. The key is to sing to them. Sirens are far less receptive to men, but if they like your song, they'll give you a chance."

"Adrian *sings*?"

Though I couldn't see her face, I somehow knew that Scarlett had rolled her eyes. "You don't have to sing well. The sirens just need to like it."

"Interesting." I paused, mind working to process the new information. "You did indeed have a reason for being out there that night."

She nodded.

"And you had your plan, this whole time?" It was a question as much as a statement of fact. Most of the pieces had fallen into place, but there were a few lingering details I still wanted answers to.

"I did—but had plenty of help." Untangling one of her arms from my grasp, Scarlett pointed to one of the men engrossed in a poker game below. "Elvira and Adrian did the heavy lifting, of course, but this one really rose to the occasion when it came time to take out the cannons at Ruiz's fort. If not for his leadership and quick thinking, there would have been far more casualties on our end of things."

Squinting, I struggled to recall the man's name; I recognized him from the bright red cap I'd never seen him without. "That's . . . Smee, correct?"

"His name is Sam, but he insisted that I call him *Mr.* Smee, which I don't understand," Scarlett said. "He's far younger than Adrian, so it's not as though he has to be formal—"

"They respect you."

"What?"

"You heard me." I squeezed Scarlett's middle, relishing our proximity. "The men respect you, perhaps more than they respect me." And why wouldn't they? Scarlett had proven herself capable and sure and had delivered on every promise she'd made. It was far more than Elvira or I could say; both of us had served as captain in the past, and neither had been afforded such unwavering loyalty during the course of our terms.

Scarlett fidgeted. "Perhaps."

"There's no reason to be modest—"

"I'm cold," she interrupted, whirling around to face me. "And there's something else I'd like to show you."

I nodded. Though bewildered at the sudden change of topic, I didn't argue. "Lead the way."

We descended the stairs and left the celebration behind, headed toward the quarters we shared. Dimly lit lanterns led the way along the cramped but familiar halls, and before long, we were alone. Scarlett busied herself with locking the door while I glanced around the room, marveling at how *normal* everything looked. Everything remained in its place, untouched and undisturbed, and it was as though the past week had been nothing more than an awful dream. My desk remained cluttered with charts and maps, our small excuse for a bed had its sheets strewn about in disarray, and even the walls still held—

Faint tinkling pulled me from my observation, and I turned

toward the sound to see Scarlett holding a small wooden object. Realizing that was where the music came from, I blinked in surprise upon recognizing it. "Where did you get that?"

"Elvira snatched it from my room prior to the ball." Crossing behind me, Scarlett placed the music box atop a stack of papers on my desk. She stared at it as it continued to play a melancholy tune, but recalling our narrow escape and how each second we'd been afforded was precious, I wasn't nearly as impressed.

"Out of everything she could have saved . . . she chose *that*?"

Scarlett shot me a glare. "I asked her to."

"Why?" Now that it was right in front of me, I could see that the music box appeared worn from either use or abuse—perhaps both. Its silver plating was tarnished, and the wood beneath had lost its luster long ago. "I'm shocked it even works."

"This isn't some broken trinket. It's enchanted to play any song asked of it. Ruiz gave it to me as an early wedding present. It seemed far too unique to leave behind, and aren't you the one always saying we need all the magical objects we can get?"

"Objects we have *use* for," I reminded her. "When are we ever going to need an enchanted music box?"

"We won't," Scarlett admitted, "but our child might."

"It's just going to take up unnecessary— *What*?" Inhaling sharply, I met her gaze before gripping the edge of the desk for support. The ship hadn't rocked any harder than normal, but it felt as though the floor had slipped out from beneath me. "You're—"

"No," Scarlett said quickly, eyes widening at the realization of what she'd implied. "There's no way. I took herbs in preparation for being with Ruiz—under no circumstances would I have let him father our child."

"Our . . . our child," I repeated, mind still reeling.

"Yes, our child." Scarlett closed the distance between us, raising a gentle hand to my cheek. "I've given this thought, Cedric. More than you might think, especially now that our curse is about to be broken, and definitely after . . ."

Any words I wanted to say fell dry on my tongue, so I waited for her to continue.

"Something happened. And no, not pregnancy, but it still forced me to take a hard look at my future. *Our* future, if you'll have me." She lifted her gaze, revealing eyes filled to the brim with tears. "I know I put you through hell back there. It wasn't fair, maybe not even right, but you stayed. You trusted me. You let me have my moment of glory, my revenge, and I felt on top of the world. It was incredible, but it was *enough*."

Scarlett paused, and somehow, I found my voice; I didn't like where this was going. "What do you mean?"

Though she was right in front of me, I barely heard her whisper. "There was a vote last night. And I won."

She didn't have to specify what. My stomach dropped, and tension melted from my shoulders, but neither were from shock— only surprise the news hadn't come sooner.

I opened my mouth to reply, but Scarlett beat me to it. "I turned it down."

"It's— You what?"

"I turned down the captaincy," Scarlett repeated. "I couldn't do that to you, not after—"

My lips found hers, swallowing whatever she had been about to say. It didn't matter. She was beautiful, she deserved this, and I'd follow her to the ends of the earth—either as her captain or *with* her as captain. I needed her to know that, even if it wasn't with words.

Scarlett surrendered completely, leaning into my touch and parting her mouth to allow me deeper access. I reached with my tongue, summoning a moan, and dragged my teeth across her lower lip before pulling away just enough to rest my forehead against hers.

"I sincerely hope you know by now," I whispered between breathless pants, "that you don't need my permission to do a damn thing. If you want this, you should claim it. I *want* you to claim it. 'Captain Maynard' has quite a nice ring to it."

She shook her head before I'd even finished. "I don't, Cedric. The only thing I want is a life with you and for you to want a life with me."

"I do," I insisted, pulling her flush against me. "I've never wanted anything more."

"Then prove it."

The parallels this conversation had to the one we'd shared on the beach weren't lost on me, but this time, I sensed sex wasn't the answer. "Anything."

Scarlett's tone turned deadly serious. "Once we piece those shards back together, once we're free of the curse, walk away. From the sea, from this ship, all of it. I don't care where we settle, but I want a home—a place where we can raise our family in peace."

My heart skipped a beat. "But Jamie—"

"Fuck Jamie. We can lose him, change our names, shed our identities—I don't care. But this chase has to *end*."

I knew then what she was asking me; if it were anyone else, I'd have allowed the flash of rage it summoned to boil over. Jamie— my brother—had spent his life trying to kill me. He'd scarred me, ridiculed me, betrayed me, and that was just the short list. She'd gotten her revenge yet expected me to forget and discard mine. Ruiz had no doubt hurt Scarlett, but they weren't bound by blood, nor had they known each other half as long. "I'm afraid it's not that simple."

"It is." Scarlett squeezed my hand. "I'm not asking you to forgive him—only to walk away."

"They may as well be one and the same," I growled. Though tempted to tear myself from her grasp, I forced myself to remain still. "He's *insane*, Scarlett, believes that time really does stand still in his so-called Neverland. That *fairies* live there, creatures no one has ever actually seen. He won't give up that delusion, nor will he give up on finding me."

"Have you ever tried, *really* tried to hide from him? Or simply made continuous excuses?"

"You know as well as I do that he won't stop until I'm dead or he is."

"So that's it, then?" Scarlett released me as her eyes flashed murderously. "You'd choose your revenge over a life with me?"

A dull ache pierced my heart at the thought of losing her. "Of course not—"

"Then what's the problem?"

"This isn't fair."

"*Answer* me, Cedric Teach—"

"You!" I finally forced; Scarlett looked as though I'd slapped her, so I quickly continued. "You're not a problem, but you're my *weakness*, Scarlett, and any children we had together would be, too. If Jamie will stop at nothing to get to me, what do you think he'd do if he found out I had a family? He already knows about you, and that's more than enough. Until he's dead, children are out of the question."

Scarlett shook her head repeatedly. "The world is massive. You're telling me there's not a single place we'd be safe?"

"From Jamie Teach? No."

"What about Neverland?" She held my gaze as if to prove her seriousness. "If he can't find it, maybe we can. Seems pretty safe to me."

"It doesn't fucking *exist*." I threw up my hands. "Jamie has been at it for years. If it were real, he would have found it by now."

She glowered. "There's got to be somewhere. Anywhere."

"He'd find us, and then we'd be on the run again. That's no life—just the illusion of one." Daring a step closer, I reached for her; though Scarlett watched me warily, she weaved her fingers through mine. "I'm not choosing him over you. If I don't end him, I'll *lose* you, and I can't have that. I won't."

She looked at me, and I honestly wasn't sure if it was irritation or longing in her gaze until she spoke. "Then marry me."

My gaze widened; of everything she could have said, I hadn't expected this.

"If we're going to face a goddamn dragon together, we may as well make it official." Scarlett began speaking faster, the words tumbling out quicker than she could enunciate them. "I know this is sudden and all we've done lately is argue, but I want you, I won't let you face this alone, and . . ."

Scarlett's voice trailed off as I sank to one knee. Swallowing hard, I took her other hand while doing my best to keep from choking up. The honest-to-gods truth was that I should have done this ages ago, so getting into position was as easy as breathing . . . but something was missing. "I don't have a ring."

She half-laughed, half-sobbed. "That's okay."

Of course it was; since when had we ever been the slightest bit traditional? Inhaling deeply, I met her tear-filled gaze, speaking more sincerely than I ever had. "All we've done from day *one* is argue, remember? You needed aboard my ship, and I needed my identity kept secret. We held each other's lives in our hands, took a chance at trusting a stranger. And look where that got us." It was my turn to chuckle. "In a whole hell of trouble, once things started to unravel. But by then, I loved you and couldn't bear to fathom a life without you."

Wetness streaked down Scarlett's cheeks. "Our fathers would fucking kill us if they knew."

"Good thing they're dead." If her father hadn't ended mine, we may well have never met. "Scarlett Ariel Maynard, will you m—"

A scream pierced the night, rattling my bones even through the locked door. Startled, Scarlett yanked herself from my grasp, reaching for the pistol at her hip while I scrambled to my feet.

"What the fuck was that?"

"Elvira," was all I managed. I wouldn't have thought my sister capable of uttering such a helpless noise, but the cry had sounded distinctly feminine, and she was the only other woman aboard the ship. Though my blood had turned to ice, my body moved of its own accord, bolting out the door, up the stairs, and back into the night.

The weather had turned for the worse. Wind howled, lightning split the sky, and waves roared beneath us as *The Jolly Serpent* rocked and churned. Keeping my balance proved a herculean task, not at all helped by the fact that the deck was soaked, and making my way toward the disturbance went much slower than I'd have liked. The Navidad festivities had clearly ended, but plenty of men remained gathered in small groups, a mixture of grim and bewildered as they shot sympathetic glances at me and Scarlett.

My heart pounded so hard it was a wonder it didn't leap from my chest, but I managed to keep my composure as I shouted to be heard over the gathering storm. "What happened? Where's Adrian?"

"Aft." Mr. Smee stepped forward, one hand on his red hat and the other gripping the rail. "That's where the scream came from. We don't know what's happened—"

"Get everyone who doesn't need to be out here below," Scarlett cut across him, her tone authoritative and direct. "Jasper, Charles, keep us steady. Mr. Smee, see to it we're not disturbed."

"Aye, Captain—er, ma'am—"

Neither of us waited to hear him finish. I'd already begun fighting my way aft to reach the stern, gritting my teeth as icy wind battered my exposed skin and chilled me to my core. I stood tall as I was able, attempting to act as a shield for Scarlett, but truth be told, I was bracing us against more than just the weather. Elvira's haunting cry hadn't ceased echoing in my mind. What in Adais's sake had happened to her, and what awaited us at the stern?

I didn't have to wait long before Adrian's shape came into view. He cradled something in his lap, and with a jolt, I realized it was my sister. Releasing my grip on the rope I'd been using for support, I half-stumbled, half-crawled toward them. Elvira's face was pale, her eyes were closed, and her body lay limp and lifeless. Fear pierced my heart, and my voice hardly sounded like my own. "Is she—"

"I'm not dead yet, you fucking bastard."

My gaze widened. "Elvira?"

"She's fine—only paralyzed with poison. Can't move anything below her neck." Adrian's voice was as hoarse as if he'd been the one screaming. "But she says she should recover in a couple 'ours."

"Naxal root," Elvira spat. "Nasty thing, but I've already built up a bit of a tolerance. I'd be helpless for a day or two without it."

I reached for her hand. "Thank the gods—"

"*No!*" Adrian hissed, but before he could pull her away, my bare fingers brushed my sister's palm; only then did I realize that there was nothing around her neck. She wasn't wearing her shard.

And I'd *touched* her.

With a cry, I stumbled back, but the damage had already been done. Elvira's whole body shuddered, but not from her doing; it was the curse taking hold, digging its roots in as deeply as it had a hold of me and Scarlett. From now on, she'd be just like us, rotting from the inside out and in constant pain, forced to kill to survive. Elvira fought to turn her head in my direction, face visibly strained. Her voice wavered as though any moment she might burst into tears, and her eyes glistened as she fought to keep them contained. "I'm so sorry, Cedric. They're gone. All the shards are gone."

"No, *I'm* sorry," I insisted. "We should have kept hold of them, we should have—"

"Cedric." Scarlett's presence enveloped me as she laid a reassuring hand on my shoulder. "It's done."

It was some time before I could speak; at least, it felt that way. Rain pelted my back until Scarlett knelt behind me, draping her arm around my shoulders and murmuring words I didn't currently care to hear. Nothing she said could change the truth or reverse what I'd done. My sister was *cursed*, but I wasn't the only one to blame.

"Jamie," I forced, voice hollow. It was the only answer that made any sense; our brother had been the only man I'd ever witnessed sneak up on Elvira. "He took them, didn't he?"

"Aye," Adrian said grimly. "Saw 'im leap back into the sea before I could do a damn thing."

"He did *what?*" Scarlett squeezed my shoulder so hard it sent pain shooting up my neck. "Where the fuck did he come from? How did he not freeze? Where's his ship?"

Adrian laughed darkly. "Are ya surprised? He is the Dragon, after all—could mean sea-dragon, for all we know. I only wish I'd have been here to stop 'im."

"It's not your fault—"

"It's mine," I cut across Scarlett. All three medallion shards, *years* of our lives . . . gone. Numbness settled in my core, and it had nothing to do with the elements that continued to mercilessly batter us. My mind spiraled for a second time. I should have kept hold of them, I should have pieced them together while I had a chance, should have—

"Cedric." Adrian's ragged voice pulled me from my thoughts. "There's somethin' else you should see."

He passed me a rolled-up piece of parchment. Though rain continued to pelt us, I opened it, not at all expecting something to tumble out. It landed on the deck with a sickening *thud*, and Scarlett screamed before scrambling back. "What *is* that?"

My best guess was a doll, but that was until I picked it up. Though no taller than my boot, it was much too heavy to be stuffed, and its limbs were stiff and far too lifelike. At its back were a pair of gossamer wings—ripped, torn, and lackluster—and its eyes were open in a piercing, horrific stare.

Adrian's mouth dropped open. "That's—"

"A fairy." The creature may have been dead, but only recently so; wherever it had come from couldn't have been far. And there was only one place fairies were rumored to exist.

I didn't dwell on the unpleasant thought as I turned my attention to the parchment. It was a thick vellum, with a map and detailed charts on one side and writing on the other. There was barely enough moonlight for me to make out the message scrawled in what was unmistakably Jamie's handwriting.

> *Second star to the right and straight on 'til morning,*
> *Follow the fairies and heed my warning:*
> *Once and for all, we'll see who wins*
> *Where After ends and Never begins.*

> *Until we meet again, brother.*
> *-J*

"Where After ends and' . . . Oh, *shit*." Scarlett squeezed again, this time digging her nails into my skin, even through my clothes. "He can't mean—"

"He does." There was only one place Jamie could be referring to: the island I swore didn't exist, the home of the fairy he'd killed to prove it. The place where time stood still, the place our feud could become eternal, and the place I feared that, as its name implied, I'd never leave. It was as real as that fairy, and whether I liked it or not, our inevitable destination.

Neverland.

THE END... BUT JUST FOR NOW!

Continue the high-seas adventure in *A Land of Never After*, where we pick up sixteen years later in Neverland.

Available now at all major retailers!

https://books2read.com/alona

For another free short story, exclusive bonus excerpts, news, and discounts, make sure to sign up for R. L. Davennor's newsletter at:

https://rldavennor.com/newsletter

ABOUT THE AUTHOR

Raelynn Davennor is an author of fantasy and science fiction, a musician and composer, and a creature of the night.

Nestled among her fictional worlds full of darkness, dragons, and sassy heroines, you'll often find a musical number or two. An accomplished performer, she's made appearances with artists such as The Who, Weird Al, and Hugh Jackman on many of the largest stages in the United States.

Raelynn is usually lost in her head, dressing up in costume, or humming a tune she can't wait to scribble down. When not obsessing over her latest idea, she enjoys pampering her menagerie of pets and pretending she isn't an adult. Her home base is https://rldavennor.com where you'll find more information, her newsletter, and links to social media.

Made in the USA
Coppell, TX
13 March 2023

14170122R00062